Kestrel Island

A.B. Martin

Cover design by ebooklaunch.com
Formatting by Polgarus Studio

www.abmartinauthor.com

For Beatrice
With love

CHAPTER 1

'OK, Jess, it's show time!' shouted Ellie, as she steered her car into the oncoming traffic and headed straight for the red car that was hurtling towards her. The two vehicles smashed together sending the red car spinning out of control, clattering into the back of Sophie's car and jolting her out of her seat. When it finally came to a halt, the three drivers roared with laughter as the music stopped and the cars finally lost their power.

It was a girls' day out at the fairground and they'd been riding the bumper cars for the last ten minutes. They'd filled their faces with hot dogs and popcorn and laughed and gasped on the twisting, turning rides.

All around them the fairground was doing a roaring trade. Stallholders were shouting, small children were squealing. Music was blasting out from every ride, the thumping bass vibrating through the air.

They clambered out of their bumper cars and stepped into the warm summer sunshine.

'We've got to go on Revolver,' said Jessica, staring up at the giant Ferris wheel that towered over the park. 'From the top, you can see right across the town.'

'Sorry girls,' said Sophie. 'The only way you'd get me to ride on that thing is if it was lying on its side.'

The girls didn't try to change Sophie's mind. They knew she didn't share their love of fear and adrenaline. Sophie preferred to keep her feet firmly planted on the ground. It was safer that way.

'Isn't that your brother up there?' said Jessica, pointing towards the top of the Ferris wheel, as it stopped to take on more passengers.

Ellie squinted up at the giant metal frame. In the cab at the top were three teenage boys, one of whom was her older brother Josh. They were joking around, waving and shouting at a group of girls who were parading down below.

'Oh no, he's with that idiot Daniel Fletcher,' said Ellie.

Daniel was the joker of the group. He was fair-haired and wiry, a mischief maker who enjoyed being the main event. When he realised the parading girls had stopped to look up, he squeezed himself under the safety harness and stood up in the cab, stretching his arms up to the bar above his head. Then he hoisted himself up into a series of pull-ups, before calmly lowering himself down again and standing triumphantly smiling at the girls down below.

Sophie's heart was in her mouth. Why would anyone take a chance on doing something so dangerous? He was such a long way up. One false move and he would plummet to his death. She felt vulnerable and frightened just looking at him.

Suddenly the cab rocked slightly, causing Daniel to lose his balance. He reached out instinctively, but before he could steady himself he'd started to topple over the side. Scrabbling and snatching at anything he could get his hands on, he just managed to grab hold of a support bar on the underside of the cab and cling on for dear life, dangling eighty feet above the ground.

Josh leaned out of the cab and tried to grasp Daniel by the wrist. It was a hot and sticky day and the sweat on his palm made it hard to keep a tight hold.

'No Josh, get back!' Ellie shouted.

One of Daniel's shoes came off and plummeted down through the wheel, clattering against a series of metal girders as it fell. Sophie gasped with horror at every thump and clunking sound the shoe made, imagining the damage those girders would do if Daniel were to slip and fall.

As a small crowd started to gather, the third boy leaned over the side and managed to get a grip on Daniel's other wrist. Together they tried to hoist him up into the cab but it was all they could do just to hang onto him. Sophie could see the strain on their faces. They looked absolutely terrified.

The operator of the ride was in a panic. He rushed back into his control booth to activate the mechanism and the massive wheel started to turn again. But as it made its slow descent, the cab was swinging and juddering making it difficult for Josh and his friend to keep a firm grip.

Gritting their teeth and straining every sinew, they clung onto Daniel as he dangled helplessly, pleading with them not to let go. Finally, when they were about ten feet above the ground they couldn't hold him any longer. He slipped from their moist and sweaty hands and fell to the ground, yelping with pain as he landed. When he tried to stand up he grasped his ankle in pain, but that was the least of his problems. The ride operator was upon him in seconds.

'What on earth do you think you were doing up there, you idiot?' he shouted.

Daniel glanced up at him dismissively.

'Chill out, dude. I slipped, that's all.'

'You slipped after you'd been swinging around like a monkey. You could have killed yourself.'

Daniel flashed a smile at the girls who had been parading down below. But they just turned and slowly walked away. The show was over. It was time to look at some of the other amusements.

Having witnessed the horror of Daniel's narrow escape, the girls didn't feel like going on Revolver anymore. They made their way out of the fairground and strolled around the park listening to Ellie rant about what an idiot Daniel Fletcher was.

'Now you know why I don't like going on Ferris wheels,' said Sophie. 'They're dangerous, he could have been killed.'

Jessica looked at her in disbelief.

'He took off his safety harness and started swinging around on the bars. Would you have done that?'

'No, I wouldn't,' said Sophie. 'But it would be just my luck that I'd do everything right and then Daniel

Fletcher's shoe would plummet down and smack me on the head.'

Ellie and Jessica burst out laughing. Sophie could always find a funny line to lift the mood.

It was a hot July afternoon and the park was scattered with people sunbathing and picnicking on the grass. Keeping a watchful eye out for Frisbees, footballs and the occasional marauding skateboarder, they sauntered around the park basking in the warm sunshine. School was out for the summer and their minds were full of possibilities.

'This weather is so amazing,' said Jessica. 'I hope it stays like this for your holiday later in the week.'

'Thanks,' said Sophie, 'but it's not really a holiday. We're just moving out of the house for a while so the builders can knock out the back wall to extend our kitchen. My dad's not even coming with us.'

'Why not?' said Ellie.

'He's worried about leaving the house empty at night. He's sleeping in a tent in the back garden and cooking his meals on a little camping stove.'

Ellie and Jessica looked at Sophie aghast.

'What?' said Ellie. 'You've got to be joking.'

'Yes, I know,' said Sophie. 'It's nuts isn't it? Now you

know how I ended up being so cautious. You should see him locking up the house whenever we go out for the afternoon. He checks everything about ten times. If a burglar did manage to break in I doubt if he'd be able to break back out again.'

A steady stream of joggers bobbed past, headphones on, bottle in hand, constantly on the lookout for overexcited dogs. From time to time a squirrel would dart down from one of the trees, find something of interest on the grass then scurry away to examine it in seclusion.

They walked over to the lake and headed for the shade of the horse chestnut trees that grew in abundance along the far bank. Little rowing boats were scattered around on the water mostly powered by overweight dads who were sweating and puffing as they tried to avoid the other boats in their path.

'Are you going to do any sailing while you're on holiday?' Jessica asked.

'I don't know,' Sophie answered. 'We're staying with my Uncle John, but I don't even know whether he's got a boat anymore.'

Sophie's Uncle John was the person who had first taught her to sail. He'd wanted to teach her when she was only four years old, but Sophie's dad wouldn't agree to it until she could swim. But the first time she stepped onto a boat she took to it immediately, and by the time she was eight she could take control of a small dinghy.

But Sophie doubted whether her uncle would have any time for sailing at the moment. Last year he and his wife Hannah bought an old hotel in Dorset and this summer was their first full season. She assumed he'd be too busy running the hotel to go larking about on the water.

'The hotel had been losing money for years when they first took it over,' said Sophie. 'Apparently, it was a bit dilapidated and ramshackle. But it looks cool on the internet. I'm really looking forward to staying there. And it will be lovely to see Uncle John again.'

'What's he like?' said Ellie.

'He's great fun,' said Sophie. 'And apparently, he was a bit of a wild man when he was younger. Had all sorts of adventures and scrapes and travelled a lot.'

'I still can't believe you're a sailor,' said Jessica. 'You won't go on a Ferris wheel but you're quite happy to be miles out at sea.'

'To be honest, Uncle John's the only person I've ever been on a boat with. He has a way of making you feel relaxed. I'm never worried when I'm with him.'

It was late in the afternoon, so they walked around to the top of the lake and started making their way back towards the town.

'Let's call into the bookshop on our way through the town,' said Ellie. 'I want to pick up that Sonja Malkin book you two have been raving about.'

'Oh, you're going to love it,' said Jessica. 'Every time I see it I always think of you.'

'Is that because it's so glamorous and exciting?' said Ellie.

'No,' said Sophie. 'It's because it's five hundred pages long so it's a bit thick.'

Ellie laughed and barged gently against Sophie's shoulder.

The bookshop was in the old part of the town. It had large windows that overlooked the piazza and big comfy armchairs to sit and read in. In the heart of the store was a small coffee shop to tempt you to stay a little longer, creating a second chance for you to buy once you'd refuelled.

Sophie never needed any persuasion to spend time in a bookshop. She'd been an avid reader as far back as she could remember, and she loved the sensation of opening a new book for the first time. It was the powdery quality of the pages. It suggested they were unsullied by the sweat of other people's hands. They felt so deliciously crisp and neat. Whenever she visited a bookshop she always tried to pick out a book from the back of the pile, hoping she was the first person who had ever set eyes on those pages. That way, it felt like a new adventure, where anything was possible.

Her favourite books were stories that took you on exciting journeys, with heroes and villains and thrilling climaxes. Sophie didn't need Ferris wheels when she could have all the excitement she wanted by escaping to another world in a book. And she had such a vivid imagination she always managed to create really distinct mental pictures of the world she was reading about. Halfway through a story, the characters would become so real to her that if one of them came to a sticky end she would often be heartbroken.

As she contemplated her trip down to Dorset later that week, Sophie thought she could use a little more excitement in her own life. She was happy living in the affluent Kentish town of Hampton Spa, but she had a nagging doubt that there must be more to life than this.

Her friends were all jetting off on exotic foreign holidays this summer. As usual, the Watsons would be holidaying in the U.K. There was often talk of the family going somewhere a little more adventurous but it never came to anything, mainly because Sophie's dad didn't like flying.

'It's not natural,' he always said. 'We're not supposed to be up there.'

Sophie's mum had tried everything to persuade him to change his mind but it never did any good. The truth was he was a bit frightened of flying but, as he was a man, he didn't like to admit it.

So now they go to the English seaside every summer. Some little town with the words 'by the Sea' or 'Bay' tagged onto the end of its name and stay at grand seafront hotels whose best days had long gone.

Sophie didn't mind this at all when she was younger. She loved the beach and could easily have stayed there all day. It was two weeks of sand, ice cream and pizza, the perfect summer break. But now she was twelve years old she was hoping they'd do something a bit more interesting this year. She wasn't expecting the Caribbean or an African safari but, let's face it, nothing exciting ever happens on an English seaside holiday.

CHAPTER 2

The hot weather continued for the rest of the week and was expected to last for some time. As Sophie and her mum set off from Hampton Spa, it was a day for light clothing and air conditioning, the perfect weather for a seaside holiday.

'I thought we'd never get away your dad was fussing so much,' said Mrs Watson. 'If he'd checked our tyre pressure one more time I think I might have locked him in his shed.'

'And where did he get those shorts from?' said Sophie. 'They look like something he used to wear when he was a teenager. Hasn't his wardrobe ever heard of the twenty-first century?'

'I don't think your dad has acclimatised to the twenty-first century yet, darling. Give him time though, he'll get there.'

'You've got to love him though,' said Sophie, chuckling.

For the first part of the journey they kept the radio on to pick up local traffic reports, but whenever the news came on it was one gloomy story after another. Inflation was up, rail strikes had been announced and the family of Nobel Prize winning scientist Julius Merrick were appealing for information on his whereabouts. He had been missing for the last three days and his wife and daughters were tearfully asking for help.

There were also worrying reports coming out of the Climate Change Conference in Stockholm, where climatologists reported that the earth was experiencing its hottest year since records began.

'This is such an important conference,' said Mrs Watson. 'If there isn't a breakthrough this week it could be very serious for the planet.'

Mrs Watson was a prominent member of the Green Party, and as Sophie grew up she was encouraged to take responsibility for the future planet she wanted to live on.

'Look after the world,' Mrs Watson always said. 'We don't have anywhere else to live.'

Sophie had totally embraced this challenge and was now a committed environmentalist, helping her mum with her campaigns and spreading the word amongst her friends.

Driving through the countryside of Surrey and Hampshire reminded Sophie what a privilege it was to live on this beautiful planet. It was the height of summer and on either side of the road the verge was lush and teeming with life. Wildflowers grew in abundance. Opening themselves up to the sky they basked in the warmth of the sun. It was a glorious feast of colour displaying a carefree, rampant enthusiasm not evident in the well-manicured gardens of the town.

The land was a patchwork quilt of fields. Some green, some yellow, some brown. Birds, butterflies and insects flitted through the air, and cows and sheep grazed lazily in the fields. From time to time, one of the cows would look up to investigate these strange metal beasts who moved past so quickly. Sophie thought they were beautiful creatures, so gentle and serene.

After travelling for about three hours they finally left the dual carriageway and turned onto the twisty little road that would take them down to Bramlington Bay. The tall hedgerows that grew up on either side of the road gave the impression they were travelling down a long tunnel. The road was so narrow that in some parts there wasn't room for two cars to pass one another safely. If they encountered a car coming from the other direction one of them would have to stop, then back up until they reached a wider part of the road so the other car could pass by.

About ten minutes after leaving the dual carriageway, a large black car suddenly appeared behind them.

'What's he up to?' said Mrs Watson, looking in her rear view mirror. 'He's going much too fast for these roads.'

Sophie turned to look at the car. The driver seemed very agitated and appeared to be shouting something at them. He was driving very close to the back of the Watson's car and kept pulling out as if he was trying to overtake.

'What's the idiot trying to do?' said Mrs Watson, sounding a little anxious. 'You can't pass on this road, there isn't room.'

At one point the two cars were almost touching, then the black car tried to overtake once more, and when this wasn't possible he flashed his lights and sounded the horn several times.

'If he gets any closer he'll be on the back seat,' Mrs

Watson shouted. 'This is insane. The fool is going to kill us.'

Sophie gripped the side of her seat and turned to look through the rear window again.

'Go back, you're too close!' she shouted.

The car was being driven by a man with dark hair wearing sunglasses. He shouted something back at Sophie and waved his arm at her aggressively. Then he sounded his horn and tried unsuccessfully to overtake again. Sophie was becoming quite distressed. This was not the start to the holiday she had hoped for.

'I'd pull over if I could but there's nowhere to stop,' shouted Mrs Watson. 'Anything to get rid of this lunatic.'

The road snaked to the right suddenly and Mrs Watson had to swing the steering wheel sharply to avoid smashing straight into a dry stone wall.

'This is madness,' she shouted, as their car weaved alarmingly from side to side.

When they went over the brow of a hill, the road seemed to widen a little and suddenly the black car was alongside them. The driver shouted some abuse at Mrs Watson and waved his arm furiously. He had an angry intensity about him and a malevolence that made Sophie recoil in fear. They thought he was going to power right past them but he didn't, he stayed level for a few seconds occasionally glancing across.

Suddenly the road started to narrow again. Still the black car was alongside them. There would never be room for both of them to get through such a narrow gap. Surely he was going to speed past or drop back. But he just stayed level, glaring across at them maliciously. Mrs Watson slammed on her brakes just in time and dropped a few feet behind him, almost colliding with a large tree on the nearside of the road. As she did the black car drove away at speed, sounding its horn several times, and disappeared around a corner.

'What a maniac,' shouted Mrs Watson. 'What on earth was he playing at? I was doing about fifty. It wouldn't have been safe to drive any faster on these roads. You can't see what's around the next corner.'

'Did you see his licence plate?' Sophie asked. 'It was RF1. I wonder what RF stands for.'

'How about Reckless Fool?' said Mrs Watson. 'The moron should be locked up.'

About a mile further down the road, they reached the outskirts of Bramlington Bay. As they passed the first few houses, they came across a large black and white sign that marked the entrance to the town.

Bramlington Bay Welcomes Safe Drivers.

Mrs Watson gave a mocking laugh.

'Well, if RF is a safe driver,' she said, 'I'd hate to see what the rest of the town are like.'

They drove down the coast road that ran the length of the seafront looking for the entrance to The Grand Hotel. It was easy to see why Bramlington Bay had been so popular in its heyday. The beautiful sandy beach stretched out in front of the town from the rocky cliffs of the Jurassic coastline to where Mawson's Rock poked out into the sea. Beyond it was the harbour where the sailing boats and pleasure crafts were moored. As soon as Sophie saw the beach, memories came flooding back to her of the lovely family holidays she had when she was younger.

Her earliest memory of the seaside was a family day trip to Brighton when she was three. As they sat on the beach eating their picnic, Sophie's dad told her that all the big hotels on the seafront were only there on their summer holidays and would have to go back to London the following week. He claimed they were all lined up along the seafront to take advantage of the sea air, before returning to the smoke and fumes of the city on Sunday. He drew Sophie some wonderful pictures of hotels in swimming trunks larking about in the sea and laying on the beach eating ice cream. They had arms and legs and happy faces and wore hats and sunglasses. Mr Watson's comic drawings always managed to make Sophie laugh.

They finally reached The Grand Hotel and it looked even more impressive than it had on the internet, with balconies that overlooked the sea and a beautiful vine growing up and around the main door. Two large palm trees stood at either side of the entrance and the hotel was a faded white colour that made it look like a majestic watering hole on some exotic little Caribbean island. A man was sitting in an open topped sports car in the car park. He was wearing a linen jacket and sunglasses and he seemed to be sketching something. He looked like a spy.

Mrs Watson reversed the car into a shaded parking spot and they carried their bags into the lobby. The inside of the hotel was just as striking. There was a wide winding staircase that seemed to go on and up forever, and sparkling chandeliers hung from the high ceiling. In the lobby, there were big comfy armchairs and copies of glamorous magazines lay invitingly on a table. A large ceiling fan spun lazily just in front of the reception area.

As they took in the splendour of it all Sophie's Aunt

Hannah came out of a small office next to the reception desk. She was bustling and busy and was carrying a large wad of papers. On seeing Sophie and Mrs Watson her face lit up. She dropped the papers on the desk and rushed out from behind it to greet them.

'Michelle, Sophie, how lovely to see you,' she said, giving them both a big hug.

'Hello Hannah,' said Mrs. Watson, smiling warmly. 'It's so nice of you to put us up like this.'

John Hodgson came running down the stairs smiling broadly. He was tall and tanned with broad shoulders and he had a confident air about him.

'I saw you arrive from one of the upstairs windows,' he said, leaning forward to give Mrs Watson a hug. 'How are you, Sis? And you too, Sophie?' he said, hugging Sophie. 'It's so good to see you both.'

'Uncle John, this place is gorgeous,' said Sophie. 'I thought you told us you'd bought a rundown hotel. This is more like a palace.'

'Thank you,' he said. 'But you might not think that if you saw some of the rooms we haven't spent any money on yet. How was your journey?'

'Well, it was alright until we came off the dual carriageway,' said Mrs Watson. 'But once we got onto that little road that runs down to the town some idiot almost killed us he was driving so close.'

'Oh no,' said Hannah. 'Are you OK?'

'We are now, but it was a terrifying experience. I had a hell of a job just trying to keep the car on the road.'

'He was driving a big black car,' said Sophie, 'with the licence plate RF1.'

A look of anger swept across John's face.

'Rupert Flynn,' he said. 'That man's a menace. Everywhere he goes there's trouble.'

'Who is he?' Sophie asked.

'He calls himself a businessman. He owns a lot of property in the area but his business methods are questionable, to say the least. People who stand up to him have a habit of being involved in accidents.'

'He nearly caused another accident this afternoon,' said Mrs Watson. 'He was like a maniac with an anger management problem.'

'Yes, that sounds like Flynn,' said John. 'Well, I'm just glad both of you are OK. Are these your bags?'

'Yes,' said Sophie, looking at the three large suitcases. 'We're travelling light.'

'If you're ready, let me show you to your rooms.'

'And I'll see you once you've settled in,' said Hannah.

'We can have a chat and do some catching up.'

John picked up the two heaviest looking suitcases and led them across the lobby to the stairs. When they reached the first floor they followed him down a corridor until he finally stopped outside room number 103.

'Here we are,' he said, putting down the suitcases with a sigh. 'You're in rooms 103 and 104.' He turned the key in the lock and pushed the door open.

The room was bathed in sunshine and through the open window all they could see was sea and sky.

'Wow,' said Sophie. 'What a view. Is this my room?'

John carried the suitcases into the room and put them down next to the bed.

'The other room is next door,' he said. 'The view is exactly the same.'

There was a door next to a large wardrobe which he pushed open and they all walked through to the other room. Sophie went to the window and looked out at the sea. He was right. The view was just as amazing.

'I'm sorry your dad couldn't make it down this time,' said John. 'Is he going to be alright on his own?'

'Oh, Dad will be OK,' said Sophie. 'He loves roughing it. He couldn't wait to get the tent out so he could sleep out in the open.'

'And the Olympics are on at the moment,' said Mrs Watson. 'Even if we had dragged him down here he'd have just sat in front of the TV all day.'

'Well, if he changes his mind he'd be very welcome.'

'Thank you, John,' said Mrs Watson. 'It's very kind of you to help us out like this.'

'I'd better let you unpack,' said John, turning to go. 'I'll leave the keys here for you. If you need anything just give me a shout.'

'Thanks, John, that's great,' said Mrs Watson. With that John left.

Gazing out at the sea view, Sophie noticed the man who had been sitting outside in a sports car. He was now on the opposite side of the road and he seemed to be taking photos of the hotel with his phone. What on earth was he doing this for? To Sophie, it all seemed very mysterious.

CHAPTER 3

Despite the long drive from Hampton Spa, Sophie wasn't at all tired. She was keen to get out and see what the rest of the hotel was like. So far she was really impressed.

'Do you mind if I go for a nose around the hotel while you're unpacking?' she said, as her mum started opening the suitcases. 'I want to see what the garden is like and find out if there's anything to do while we're down here.'

'Alright darling,' said Mrs Watson. 'But take your phone with you and don't stray too far, will you?'

Slipping the phone into her pocket, she left the room and made her way down the stairs towards the lobby. A few stragglers from lunch were still lingering in the bistro. They were in high spirits and had obviously feasted well. Sophie smiled at one of the staff who was patiently waiting for them to finish, then pushed the door open and stepped out into the garden.

There was a paved area immediately outside the door where a collection of tables and chairs were set out for al fresco dining. The rest of the garden was given over to a beautiful lawn which was surrounded by several large trees, including a magnificent willow tree whose branches draped lazily in the sunshine. An elderly couple were sitting on a bench under the willow. It looked such a peaceful spot. Sophie thought it would be the perfect place for a little afternoon reading.

'Lovely old tree isn't it?' said John, suddenly appearing from the door behind her.

'It's a lovely garden,' said Sophie. 'It must be amazing to own such a beautiful hotel.'

'Well, it will be eventually,' he answered. 'But there's a lot of work to do before we reach that stage. Would you like a tour?'

'Yes please,' said Sophie, 'if you have the time to spare.'

'Of course I have,' said John.

They spent the next half hour touring around the hotel. Sophie saw the new kitchen that had been installed at great expense and sampled some of the sweet treats they were preparing for dinner that evening. Lemon tart, chocolate fudge cake, delicious teaspoonfuls of their homemade ice cream. It was a carnival for her taste buds and she found it hard to tear herself away.

The kitchen was a hive of activity. It was mid afternoon and the staff were painstakingly cleaning down all the work surfaces after a busy lunchtime session. There was a smell of disinfectant in the air as an elderly man mopped the floors vigorously. He smiled at Sophie as she passed.

'Floors are a bit slippery, madam,' he said. 'Careful how you go.'

John also showed Sophie his plans for an extension that would double the size of the bistro and create space for the hotel to host wedding receptions and conferences.

Finally, he took her up to the part of the hotel that was still waiting to be refurbished. The bottom of the stairs had been roped off to the public and the steps creaked and wobbled a little as they carefully climbed up. The carpet was worn and threadbare and the walls looked as if the colour had been washed out of them a long time ago. High up in a corner a silky cobweb swayed slightly as they passed. It had been a few years since paying customers had walked up these stairs.

'If business is good this summer, we're hoping to refurbish this part of the hotel during the winter months,' said John. 'The staircase needs to be replaced and the three rooms need a complete overhaul.'

At the top of the stairs Sophie paused for a moment when a strange shiver went down her spine.

John noticed her discomfort.

'It's a bit spooky up here, isn't it?' he said.

'Yes,' she answered. 'It's like an old haunted house.'

'Well, it's funny you should say that. Some of the older staff say they've seen some strange sights up here, tricks of the light and fleeting images mostly. Apparently, it's very weird when it happens.'

'Do you mean they've seen ghosts?' she said, looking a little concerned.

'Well no, I wouldn't call them ghosts. More like strange lights and images.'

Sophie stopped and started edging back towards the stairs.

'I'm not really sure I want to see this bit,' she said. 'I'm finding it all a bit creepy.'

'Oh no, I'm so sorry,' said John. 'I wasn't trying to freak you out. Honestly, there's nothing to worry about. I've never seen anything up here.'

Sophie still wasn't convinced. She could feel herself starting to tense up. She glanced down the stairs. The floor down below seemed so safe and cosy.

'Look, let me show you one of the rooms,' he said, smiling at her. 'They're big, bright rooms and it's the middle of the afternoon. I promise you'll be OK.'

Something about his manner and his self assurance seemed to calm her fears.

'OK,' she said. 'Sorry I'm such a wimp.'

He pushed open the first door they came to and walked inside. Sophie could see what a big job he had on his hands. The room was empty of furniture and it smelled a bit stale and musty. It looked like it hadn't been occupied for years. The wallpaper was peeling and cracked, there were horrible stains on the carpet and the light fitting was just bare wires hanging out of the ceiling.

On seeing the room Sophie's discomfort started to return. It looked abandoned, almost as if people were keeping well away from it. She felt like running away herself.

But as John described how the finished room would look, Sophie tried to picture the scene he painted. Plush carpets and curtains, a king-size bed and a sumptuous sofa for guests to recline and relax on. It all sounded very inviting. There was also a magnificent view across the top of the trees in the back garden. The willow tree swaying peacefully in the gentle breeze was such a beautiful sight. John was right. It would be a lovely room when it was finished. Sophie was really impressed.

But as she turned away from the window something truly extraordinary happened. Strange lights appeared in the room, flickered for a moment then disappeared. When they returned a few seconds later they were brighter and more plentiful, dancing around the room as if they were being orchestrated.

'What on earth….?' said John.

Sophie felt a flash of alarm. Their talk of ghosts a few minutes ago had really spooked her and now she could feel her fear taking over again. She stood open mouthed wondering what this strange spectacle was. They were all around her and they were gathering speed, flashing and twinkling then instantly melting away. Soon they were appearing and disappearing at such an incredible rate that she was becoming quite disorientated. She could feel herself starting to shake.

She heard the distant roar of something that sounded like the howling wind. As each second ticked by it got louder and louder. The flickering lights intensified still further and the windows started to vibrate. She could hear them rattling in their aged frames. Sophie was now in panic mode.

'What's happening Uncle John?' she shouted. 'I don't like it. I'm frightened.'

John was standing wide eyed looking all around the room. Sophie wanted to run over to him but she was rooted to the spot. The roar of the wind became louder and louder. Outside it was a calm and sunny day, but in this abandoned room Sophie felt like she was being buffeted around by a gale-force wind. She leaned back against the wall in an effort to stay on her feet.

Then, just as the flashing lights were reaching a crescendo, they all hurtled towards a spot in the middle of the room and, in an explosion of lights and sound, a teenage girl materialised out of nowhere. She landed in the room as if she had manifested out of thin air, took a couple of steps to steady herself, then leapt back when she saw Sophie and John looking at her.

Sophie was barely able to believe what she was seeing. She rushed across to where John stood, her heart beating so fast she thought it might burst out of her chest. She could sense that John was just as shocked. His body had tensed as he braced himself for a fight.

The girl looked strong and athletic. She had dark hair and she wore an expression of fierce determination. Her trousers were tucked into dark brown boots and there was a large rucksack strapped to her back. She stared at John intently, studying his face with a penetrating gaze, then her shoulders went down and she relaxed a little.

'Are you John Hodgson?' she said eventually.

John stared at her for a few seconds, still ready to attack at any moment.

'Who are you?' he shouted. 'And what are you doing here?'

'My name is Sienna,' she said. 'My father said I should look for you when I arrive. He said you could help me with my quest.'

'What quest?' said John, 'and who is your father?'

'His name is Memphis,' she answered. 'He hopes you remember him from a long time ago.'

Sophie immediately felt the muscles in John's body release their tension. He took a deep breath and stared at the girl in disbelief. Then a smile started to spread across his face. It took him a few seconds to answer.

'Of course I remember your father,' he said. 'How could I ever forget him? He saved my life.'

'A long time has passed since he was here,' said Sienna. 'He was worried that you might have forgotten him. He asked me to give you this, in case I needed to jog your memory.'

She handed John a folded piece of card. Sophie peered around from behind his back as he opened it up. Inside was an old photograph of two young men on a sailing craft out at sea. They were tanned and smiling and they looked totally carefree. One of them was a young John Hodgson and the other was a long haired Adonis called Memphis. John stared at the photo for several seconds lost in the memory of those glorious times. He smiled at Sienna and studied her face.

'You have your father's eyes,' he said, handing the photograph back to her.

Sophie was still frozen with fear. She couldn't understand why John didn't seem at all concerned at these extraordinary events. In fact he was acting as if this was all perfectly normal, which it most certainly wasn't.

'What's going on Uncle John?' she said.

'Ah,' said John. 'I'm afraid this is going to take a bit of explaining.'

'Is this your daughter?' Sienna asked. Her dark eyes seemed to penetrate Sophie's soul.

'No, this is Sophie. She's my niece,' he answered. 'She's staying with me for a while.'

Sophie tried to say something to Sienna but no words came out. She just stood there staring blankly, still trembling at the sight of the new arrival.

Sienna slipped the rucksack off her back and took out a bottle of water.

'What is this place?' she asked, looking around the room.

'It's a hotel,' said John. 'Well, the other parts of the building are. We're still working on this room.'

She took a few sips of water then put the bottle back into her rucksack.

'You say you are on a quest,' said John. 'What is it you're looking for?'

'I'm searching for The Orb of Nendaro,' Sienna answered. 'It was stolen from my father by a dissident troublemaker called Osorio. He's been trying to seize power and my father thinks he's fled to your world to develop his plans.'

'And how can I help you?'

'I'm going to need somewhere to stay,' she said. 'And I'll need some help understanding how things work in this world.'

'I have a room on the second floor you can stay in,' said John, 'and I'll be happy to help you with anything else you need.'

'Thank you,' Sienna answered.

John knew that Sienna's journey would have taken a lot out of her.

'You must be tired,' he said.

She nodded and slipped the rucksack back onto her shoulder.

Sophie was standing quietly to one side, still alarmed by what she was witnessing. John could sense her apprehension.

'I know this all seems a bit strange, Sophie,' he said, 'but please don't be concerned. I'll explain everything to you once Sienna has settled in.'

Sophie didn't respond. It was difficult to know what to say. She just followed John and Sienna as they moved towards the door.

They went down to the second floor where John showed Sienna to a room that overlooked the garden. It was small and neat and suited her perfectly. The impact of her journey was now starting to show. She slumped down onto the bed and exhaled loudly.

'I have an office on the ground floor,' said John.

'Once you've had a chance to rest, come down to see me and we'll talk more about how I can help.'

Sophie was relieved to be able to close the door and leave Sienna to rest. This strange episode had alarmed and unnerved her, and she desperately needed an explanation from John. What was going on? How could someone just appear out of nowhere? Sophie needed some answers.

CHAPTER 4

As they made their way down the winding staircase towards the ground floor, there was an uneasy tension between them. John was still trying to sound relaxed and matter of fact but Sophie was very much on edge. She wasn't comfortable with the weird and unknown. She liked certainty and the things she was familiar with.

Once they were in his office, John closed the door and asked Sophie to sit in the chair by his desk.

'So,' he said. 'I think I owe you an explanation about what's going on here.'

He paused for a moment to gather his thoughts, unsure of what to say.

'What I'm going to tell you might seem a bit far-fetched,' he said, 'but I swear it's as much of the truth as I know.'

He paused again as if looking for the right words.

Finally, he just came out and said it.

'Sienna is not from this world,' he said. 'She comes from a different place, a parallel world to ours called Galacdros.'

Sophie just stared at him for a few seconds, unable to take in what she had heard.

'A parallel world?' she said, looking a bit puzzled. 'What's a parallel world?'

'It's a world that's quite a lot like ours, but it exists in a different universe. Occasionally these worlds bleed into one another and cause people to see strange images and shapes, but most of the time they operate completely independently.'

Sophie looked shocked.

'So is Sienna an alien?' she asked tentatively.

'Well, she's not an alien in a 'little green man from Mars' way,' he answered. 'But she's not from this planet. Our worlds operate in the same time and space but in a different dimension.'

'Sorry,' she said. 'I'm afraid I still don't understand. This is all just a bit too freaky.'

'I know it must sound weird,' said John, 'and to be honest, I don't really understand the physics of it all myself. All I know is the two worlds co-exist and, at a certain level, cooperate with one another but for security reasons it's not something that's general knowledge.'

'So how did Sienna get here?' she asked.

'Well, there are a small number of portals where it's possible to travel between the two worlds but it requires immense skill and power. I can only assume Sienna had help from her father to come here today. He is an extraordinary individual and has travelled between our worlds on several occasions.'

There was a look of pained confusion on Sophie's face. She didn't want to believe any of this. It all seemed too fantastical.

'I realise this all sounds totally incredible,' said John. 'It took me a while to take it all in.'

To Sophie it was more than incredible, it was mind blowing. She'd just watched someone from another world appear in the room out of thin air. And within seconds John was acting as if it was perfectly normal. In fact, there was a photograph from many years ago of John with this strange girl's father. So what else did he know about her world?

'She said that you knew her father when you were younger.'

'Yes,' said John. 'He was asked to come here to assist

in the security of our planet. Memphis is a highly skilled telepath and mind reader and he came here to try to teach his techniques to the security services.'

'So how did you meet him?' Sophie asked.

'I was one of his students,' said John.

Sophie was flabbergasted.

'You were in the security services?' she said. 'You were in MI5?'

'Well, let's just say I was one of the agents Memphis was assigned to teach.'

'Wow! Does Mum know about this?'

'No, I've never told any of my family apart from Hannah. And in case you're wondering, I'm not a very good telepath either. Unfortunately, I was a terrible student and never got the hang of it at all. But Memphis and I always enjoyed each other's company and after he'd finished his assignment I travelled with him for a couple of months. He wanted to look around our planet, have a few adventures before he went home. We had a lot of fun together and got up to the odd bit of mischief, and towards the end of our travels he saved my life.'

'He saved your life? What happened?'

'We were staying in Florida and had taken a small boat out to enjoy the ocean,' said John. 'It was a warm and sunny day, so being young and reckless I took off my shirt and dived into the water for a swim. I didn't see the shark until it was too late. It took my leg and dragged me under the water. It happened so suddenly I didn't understand what was going on. All I knew was the pain was unbearable. When it let go I realised what had happened, but I was losing a lot of blood and was struggling to get back to the boat. Then it turned and came back for a second bite.

Memphis was in the water beside me by the time the shark arrived. He sunk his knife deep into the creature's nose and it retreated to a safe distance for a moment. In those few seconds Memphis was able to drag me back to the boat and one of the crew helped to get me back on board. Then the shark moved in again, but Memphis was an immensely powerful man and as it struck he landed a heavy blow on the side of the creature's head. It didn't come back for another try.'

'I'm surprised you could ever get back on a boat after that,' said Sophie. 'If that happened to me I wouldn't even go back on the beach.'

'Well, shark attacks are actually quite rare,' said John. 'It's only in books and movies that they happen all the time. I just got unlucky.'

'So are there seas and oceans in this other world then? I mean, Memphis seemed to know exactly what to do.'

'Apparently, his world is not that different to ours,' John answered. 'The oceans, the terrain, the plant life and even the weather are quite similar. It took him no time at all to adapt to our culture.'

Sophie sat and thought for a minute, trying to take in the enormity of everything she had heard. She stared at the floor and shook her head with astonishment. So there are other worlds out there. And in some of these worlds there are people who look quite a lot like us.

Her thoughts were interrupted when she felt her phone vibrate in her pocket. It was a text from her mum. She quickly thumbed in a response.

'Is everything OK?' said John.

'Yes, it's just Mum,' she answered. 'She was wondering where I was. I said I'd meet her in the garden.'

They left the office and strolled out to the garden to wait for Mrs Watson.

'Don't worry about any of this,' said John. 'It probably won't affect you at all. Sienna seems to be on some sort of mission, so the chances are she won't be here that long. You just concentrate on having fun and enjoying your holiday.'

'I'll try,' she said, 'but you have to admit, it's totally weird.'

'Yes it is,' he answered. 'It's incredibly weird.'

He smiled at her, hoping to be able to give a little reassurance.

'By the way,' he said, 'I've got a little boat called Betsy tied up in the moorings near the Harbour Cafe. I'm not getting the chance to use it much at the moment, but while you're down here you're welcome to take it out any time you want.'

'Thanks, Uncle John. But I've never actually taken a boat out on my own before.'

'You could have gone out on your own by the time you were nine years old,' he said. 'You're a natural sailor.'

CHAPTER 5

The following morning, Sophie woke early to the sound of seagulls screeching to one another high above the hotel. It sounded as if they were sending high pitched 'good mornings' all around the town. She looked at her watch. It was only seven thirty. On a school day she would be sleepily shovelling in her breakfast at this time of day, but as she was on holiday it was much too early to get up. She lay in bed and enjoyed the warmth and comfort of a lazy start to the morning. Breakfast was served until ten. There was no need to get up just yet.

But her sense of comfort and security was shattered, when she suddenly thought of Sienna. There was an alien in the hotel, someone from another world. She found the thought of it really creepy. This was not what she'd expected when she left Hampton Spa the previous day.

She wondered if Sienna had slept well. Did people from her world even need sleep? They obviously need water because she remembered Sienna drinking from a bottle yesterday afternoon. Sophie found the idea of sharing a hotel with her really weird. And she thought it was even weirder that John seemed to be unfazed by Sienna's story. To think that people from another world were walking around this planet and yet most people didn't even know. Sophie's parents knew nothing about them, nor did the school.

What should she do if she came across Sienna in the hotel? Would it be OK to touch her? What would that feel like? And how many other aliens had she encountered in the twelve years she'd been alive and not even realised who they were?

A pile of her books were stacked up by the side of the bed. They were filled with strange stories, epic fantasies and fantastic characters. When she read about the heroes of her books encountering extraterrestrials, it seemed perfectly plausible and natural. They formed friendships and alliances and triumphed over evil. But the reality of meeting someone from another world was a bit more daunting. Perhaps these things were best left to books.

All through breakfast Sophie was on the lookout just

in case Sienna came into the hotel bistro. She was only half listening to a story her mum was telling her, and her head jerked towards the door every time someone came in.

'Are you alright darling?' said Mrs Watson. 'You seem a little distracted.'

'Yes, I'm fine Mum,' she answered, 'I just slept badly.'

The truth was Sophie couldn't wait to get out of the hotel for the morning. She was keen to have a good look around the town but just as keen to avoid bumping into Sienna. She was also in two minds about whether she should tell her mum the truth about Sienna. John had never told anyone but Hannah that he used to be in MI5. If Sophie told her mum the whole story, would she be betraying his trust?

There was a lot of activity in the town that morning as Sophie and her mum strolled around taking in the sights. It was hot and sunny and the High Street was bustling with energy and noise. The small car park was closed to traffic for the day and in its place a farmers market was now in full swing. Handmade breads and cheeses were available to sample, and the local people sold jams and chutneys plus a vast array of locally grown vegetables. The smell of fried onions from the veggie burger stand wafted through the air. It mingled with the sweet smell of handmade soaps and the aroma of freshly made coffee.

A middle aged man was sitting on an upturned beer crate playing jazz music on a small saxophone, accompanied by a pre-recorded soundtrack. Sophie and her mum stopped and listened for a while entranced by the beautiful music he was creating. Before they moved away Mrs Watson put some money in his hat. The saxophonist paused in mid song to smile and thank her.

Outside the station, a group of people were milling around carrying placards and a banner. They were chanting slogans and handing leaflets to passers by.

'Hands off Kestrel Island!' one of them shouted.

Sophie took a leaflet and read the first few lines. The local people were campaigning against the development of a nearby island that was home to some rare birds and wildflowers.

'Hello ladies,' a man said as Sophie and her mum walked past. 'Would you like to sign our petition to stop the destruction of Kestrel Island?'

'What's Kestrel Island?' Mrs Watson asked.

'It's a small island just off the coast near here. The council have given permission for some industrial warehousing and a manufacturing plant to be built there, and we're concerned that it will affect the delicate eco system.'

'How awful,' said Mrs Watson.

'Would you like to sign our petition?' he asked. 'We could use all the help we can get.'

'I certainly will sign,' she said. 'Are you going to sign as well Sophie?'

They signed the petition and the man gave them both a large sticker which they wore proudly as they walked around the town. They were very happy to display their support for the local people in their campaign. Many of the shops they went into had a large poster in their window to show their support for the campaign. The whole town seemed to be behind what the protesters were doing.

'Shall we walk over the bridge to the harbour?' said Sophie.

'Why not,' said Mrs Watson. 'It's such a lovely day.'

There were more posters on show in the shops of the old harbour, where the sailing boats and pleasure cruisers rubbed shoulders as they bobbed up and down on the swell. Tourists with sun hats and rucksacks queued up to buy tickets for a tour around the bay, and a lone street performer on a very tall unicycle was bravely trying to negotiate the poorly put together cobbled street.

When they'd seen most of what the town had to offer, they stopped at a little cafe in Station Road, opposite the site where the protesters had gathered. The man they had spoken to earlier spotted them sitting outside in the sunshine and gave them the thumbs up. They responded in kind.

'He obviously remembers us from earlier,' said Mrs Watson. 'He's very good at drumming up support isn't he?'

Sophie was reading the leaflet one of the protesters had given her earlier.

'This is terrible,' she said.

'What's that darling?'

'Up until two years ago, the island was owned by an elderly lady who had devoted her life to protecting the local wildlife. She only let people visit if it was pre-arranged and the visitors agreed to keep to certain areas. But when she died her family had to sell the land to pay off her debts and the council gave the new owner permission to build there. According to this leaflet, it will destroy the habitat of some very rare species.'

'I wonder if the local Green Party are involved,' said Mrs Watson.

'Maybe that's them across the road,' said Sophie.

As she finished speaking, the man they had spoken to earlier crossed the road and came over to where they were sitting.

'I'm sorry to interrupt you ladies,' he said, then he turned to Mrs Watson, 'but I've just remembered where I've seen you before.'

'Really?' she said, looking surprised.

'I'm sure I heard you speak at a fringe meeting at the Green Party conference last year. You're Michelle Watson aren't you?'

'Yes, that's right,' said Mrs Watson, looking even more surprised.

'I'm Mike Tindall,' said the man, holding out his hand. 'I'm the Chair of the local Green Party.'

Mrs Watson shook his hand and invited him to join them.

'This is my daughter Sophie,' she said as he sat down. 'She's just been reading to me from your leaflet. This sounds terrible. I'm not surprised you're trying to fight it.'

'Well, unfortunately that's not the worst of it,' said Mike. 'The person who bought the island is a local businessman called Rupert Flynn....'

'Oh, not him again,' said Mrs Watson.

'You've heard of him then?'

'Yes, we had a run in with him yesterday. What an unpleasant man he is.'

'He's worse than unpleasant, he's a crook,' said Mike. 'Obviously we can't print this on our leaflets, but when Kestrel Island was sold the family were given verbal assurances from the council that nothing would be done to harm its delicate eco system. But Flynn has a way of influencing the council to get his own way. Threats, bribery, blackmail. It's all the same to him. He's been getting away with it for years. I'd call him a gangster but he'd be in a gang of one.'

'Do you have any idea what he's doing on the island?' Sophie asked.

'I'm afraid not. He has guards patrolling the perimeter in a speedboat, and some elderly birdwatchers who sneaked onto the west side a few weeks ago were roughed up before they were let go. We're having a meeting at the library tonight in preparation for a protest outside the town hall tomorrow. If you're not busy you'd be very welcome.'

Mrs Watson and Sophie looked at one another and hesitated.

'No need to decide now,' said Mike. 'The library is just around this corner on East Street. We'll be starting at eight and you'd both be very welcome.'

With that he shook hands with them both and returned to the protesters on the other side of the road.

'Wow, Mum,' said Sophie. 'So Mr Tindall has seen you perform has he? It's like I'm having coffee with Justin Beiber.'

As Sophie and her mum were finishing their drinks, a man sat down at the table next to them. Sophie recognised him immediately. He was the man who had been sitting outside in his car when they first arrived at the hotel. He took out his phone and pretended to be reading something, but she could see what he was really doing. He was taking photographs of the protesters, lots of them. When he noticed Sophie was looking at him, he pretended to scroll a few times, then he reluctantly put his phone away.

CHAPTER 6

After lunch, Mrs Watson decided to take a nap. It was a warm afternoon, so Sophie thought this was a perfect opportunity to do a spot of reading in the garden. The lovely old willow tree with the bench underneath would be ideal. She could sit and read, listen to the birds and let the gentle afternoon breeze cool her down.

When she reached the back door of the hotel the garden looked really inviting. Lush and green, and elegantly manicured, it seemed such a peaceful place to spend the afternoon. But as she was about to push the door open, she noticed someone sitting in the al fresco dining area. It was Sienna. She had her back to the door and there was a pile of books stacked up next to her on the table. Sophie ducked back inside unsure what she should do next.

What bad luck. If she went outside it would be

awkward if she didn't say hello, but all Sophie really wanted to do was sit quietly and enjoy her book. A wave of frustration swept through her. Is this what the holiday was going to be like? Every time she wanted to do something she'd have to check whether this strange girl was there? She shook her head in disappointment and started walking back towards the stairs.

But when she reached the lobby, Sophie paused for a moment. Why was she so worried about encountering Sienna? Was it because she was different? There's nothing wrong with being different. She thought about her last term at school and how Emma Castle and her friends had been so horrible to her. Sophie had never given them any reason to dislike her other than the fact that she wasn't the same as them. Is this what she was doing to Sienna? She paused for a moment, wondering what she should do.

Maybe Sienna wouldn't want to talk to her anyway. She might be busy. It would be perfectly possible to just say hello and exchange a few pleasantries, then walk over to the willow tree to read. She ought to at least give it a try. Walking towards the door her mouth felt dry. She tried to swallow but there was no saliva. She stopped for a few seconds at the door, entertaining fleeting second thoughts, then pushed it open and walked out into the sunshine.

The warmth of the afternoon sun hit her as soon as she stepped into the garden. It was the hottest point of the day and the flag stones were warm under her feet. When she reached the table Sienna turned and smiled at her.

'Hello,' she said, putting her book down. 'I was just looking at some maps of the area, trying to work out where we are.'

'I think we're in the garden,' said Sophie, smiling back at her.

'Erm, yes,' said Sienna, looking a bit confused.

Sophie immediately regretted her attempt at a joke. What a stupid thing to say. Sienna must think she's some sort of simpleton. Of course we're in the garden.

'Would you like some water?' said Sienna.

There was a large jug on the table filled with water and ice. It was surrounded by four glasses. Sophie hesitated. It was a hot afternoon and the water looked really inviting, but did she want to drink from a glass that Sienna might have been touching? She glanced at Sienna's hands. They looked quite normal.

'Help yourself,' said Sienna, 'it's still lovely and cold.'

Sophie hesitated, then poured herself a glass of water and took a long drink. Cradling the glass and smiling, she stood there wondering what to do next. She wanted to walk over to the willow tree and get on with her reading but that might be rude. Having just drunk some of Sienna's water she couldn't just walk away.

'Do you mind if I join you?' she said reluctantly.

'Not at all,' said Sienna. 'Please do. And help yourself to more water.'

She plonked herself down in a chair and put her book on the table beside her. In the warm summer sunshine, Sienna looked refreshed and vibrant. She was lean and athletic and she emitted a sense of raw power. Sophie found it all a bit intimidating.

'This must be strange for you,' said Sienna.

'What's strange?' Sophie answered, pretending not to know.

'To suddenly be confronted with someone from another world. I've known about your world since I was a little girl because of my father's travels. But I'm assuming that until yesterday you never knew we existed.'

'To be honest, it was a bit of a shock,' said Sophie. 'It still is. I can't even get my dad to take a plane to

Barcelona, so I was a bit alarmed when Uncle John told me you came here from a parallel world. It's quite difficult to take in.'

'I'm not that different from you,' said Sienna. 'I just grew up in another world.'

'So how come you can speak English then?' Sophie asked. 'Does everyone in Galacdros speak English?'

'No, we have our own language,' said Sienna, smiling, 'but when I was assigned to this mission I had a microchip installed in my brain that makes it possible for me to speak and understand your language. And we don't call our world Galacdros either. That's just what your leaders call it.'

'What do you call it?' Sophie asked.

'The closest translation I could give you is *Earth*,' Sienna answered.

Sophie felt a little foolish. Of course it's called Earth. How could it have been anything else?

'So what did your father tell you about us?' Sophie asked. 'Did he warn you about twelve year old girls who make stupid jokes?'

'I'm sorry. I don't understand,' said Sienna.

'My joke a minute ago,' said Sophie. 'When you said you were trying to work out where we were.'

Once again Sophie wished she hadn't started this train of conversation. If only she could begin this whole encounter again.

'Oh I see,' said Sienna. 'No. He didn't really tell me much about this world at all. Most of what he told me was to do with how I should conduct myself while I'm here. He's known in our world for his courage and his impeccable spirit, and he has always impressed upon me that I should strive for the same standards.'

'No pressure then,' said Sophie, attempting a smile.

'Does your father demand a lot from you?' Sienna asked.

'Well, no,' said Sophie. 'My dad's not really the adventurous type. At the moment he's probably sitting in a tent in our back garden eating baked beans out of a tin. His main concern is making sure the builders don't make too much of a mess of our garden.'

Sienna smiled.

'That's probably an adventure for him though,' she said.

Sophie returned Sienna's smile.

'Yes, it probably is,' she said.

She thought of her dad going around the house once the builders had gone home, scribbling things onto his clipboard and making a list of points to bring up with them the following day. He was crazy, but she loved him.

'Are you close to your father?' Sophie asked.

'Well, it's getting better,' said Sienna. 'When I was young I always thought my father was disappointed that I wasn't a boy, but I think that all started to change when I succeeded in The Coming of Age.'

'The Coming of Age?' said Sophie. 'What's that?'

'It's an annual survival challenge for students who have reached the age of sixteen. We had to survive in the wilderness for ten days eating and drinking only what we could find for ourselves. Then on the tenth day, when we were weak with hunger, we had to make it back to the command post, evade the guards and gain access to the central courtyard. Very few made it back without being apprehended. I was one of the few.'

'Wow!' said Sophie, looking visibly impressed.

'As a result, I was offered a chance to attend The Academy, a training school for our security services. It's a great honour, but it's a very tough school. Less than a tenth of those who are offered a place will graduate.'

This all sounded shockingly severe to Sophie. The toughest challenges she'd ever had to face were her piano and ballet exams, and they were nerve wracking enough. What Sienna had achieved sounded truly remarkable. Sophie couldn't imagine taking on something so demanding.

Sienna talked of her time at The Academy. The long hours of training and the skills she had to master. There were daily lessons in unarmed combat, firearms training and the psychology of war. Many of the cadets dropped out during the gruelling physical challenges that took place in jungle or desert settings. But Sienna was fuelled by a determination to succeed no matter what. She was the daughter of Memphis. She could do no less.

When she graduated she was invited to join The Elite, a secret counter terrorism force in which her father had served with great distinction. She was the youngest recruit in the force's history and this was her first mission.

Sophie listened intently, completely forgetting about her earlier fears. Sienna was a formidable and determined character and had lived such a different life to the peaceful existence Sophie enjoyed in Hampton Spa. The story of her dedication and tenacity was fascinating, and Sophie was happy to sit and listen.

'To be honest,' said Sienna, 'I don't think it was just my achievements at The Academy that got me the job.

I think they were also interested in exploiting my psychic abilities.'

'Psychic abilities?' said Sophie, looking a little shocked. 'Are you psychic?'

'My father is a well known telepath and mind reader. Lots of people in our world have these abilities. He's been teaching me since I was very young.'

'So can you read my mind?' Sophie asked.

'If I need to,' said Sienna. 'To do it without good reason would be intrusive, like opening someone's mail. But when I first met you and John at the top of the hotel I was able to read both your minds and I realised immediately that you weren't a threat to me.'

'Wow!' said Sophie. 'I'd better be careful what I'm thinking about.'

'Don't worry,' said Sienna, 'I don't do it constantly. That would be exhausting.'

Sophie suddenly remembered what she was thinking about when she entered the garden. She hoped Sienna hadn't picked any of that up. Was she aware of what Sophie was thinking now? She decided to quickly put it out of her mind and change the subject.

'When we first met, you said you were searching for something that was stolen from your father.'

'Yes,' Sienna answered. 'The Orb of Nendaro. It's a small precious stone that was taken by a dissident troublemaker called Osorio.'

'Why did he take it?' Sophie asked.

'He believes that by possessing The Orb he can absorb its special powers and gain extraordinary gifts like superhuman strength or the ability to see the future. Osorio is not a peaceful man and with these abilities he could inspire others to follow him.'

'But how can a precious stone contain these powers?' Sophie asked.

'It was once owned by Nendaro, a powerful leader who lived over five hundred years ago. Some people claim he came from the stars. He carried The Orb with him wherever he went and his followers believe that after he died it retained his essence. They say the longer a person can retain possession of it, the more powerful he could become. So it's imperative that I find Osorio without delay.'

The girls sat and talked for over an hour and the books just sat on the table. Sophie tried to limit her attempts at any more humour, and Sienna talked at length about her life back at home and how she had prepared for The Coming of Age.

Sophie hung on every word as if she was devouring one of the adventure stories she loves to read so much. Sienna was like the Warrior Queen in an A.V. Simpson book. She was courageous and powerful and unlike any other girl Sophie had ever met.

When Sienna's father found out she'd been invited to join The Elite, he was so proud he presented her with a hunting knife. It had an ornate handle carved with the family crest and it was her prized possession, a symbol of the bond she now shared with him.

'So, do you enjoy hunting?' Sophie asked.

'I don't know,' said Sienna, 'I've never actually hunted anything. I only learned all those skills so I could graduate from The Academy.'

'But why did your father give you a hunting knife then?'

'I suppose it was his way of showing me that he thinks I'm as good as any boy.'

She reached into her rucksack and took out something wrapped in a silken fabric. Inside was the knife. It had a beautifully carved handle and it looked like it had never been used.

'My father must have watched me throwing a knife at the target behind our house. I can split an apple from about twenty feet away.'

'Wow!' said Sophie. 'I'll remember that next time I'm rustling up a fruit salad.'

Sienna just stared at her looking a bit confused.

'Sorry about that,' said Sophie. 'I'm afraid that was another pathetic attempt at humour. I think I'll give my funny bone the rest of the day off.'

Before Sienna could answer, Mrs Watson and John appeared at the back door of the hotel. When they noticed the girls sitting at the table, they walked across the patio to join them.

'I hope you haven't been sitting out here for long Sophie darling,' said Mrs Watson. 'You'll bake in this heat.'

'Oh, hi mum,' said Sophie. 'This is Sienna. She's staying at the hotel at the moment.'

'Very nice to meet you, Sienna,' said Mrs Watson.

'And you too,' said Sienna, reaching out to shake Mrs Watson's hand.

'Yes, Sienna's going to be staying here for a while,' said John, seeming uncharacteristically nervous. 'Her father is an old friend of mine, and he asked if Sienna could visit for the summer to get to know the area a bit better.'

'How lovely,' said Mrs Watson. 'And you two girls

seem to be getting on very well together. It seems like perfect timing.'

It was true. Sophie may have been nervous and even a bit scared when she first ventured out into the garden, but now that she had spent some time with Sienna she had become totally captivated by her. A sixteen year old girl who had travelled to another world to avenge a crime against her family? This was the stuff of fantasy novels.

CHAPTER 7

The people of the town gathered at the library that evening to plan the next stage of their campaign. Having met Mike Tindall earlier in the day, Sophie and her mum had decided to attend the meeting. They really wanted to show their support.

'I wonder if there's anything about the island online,' said Sophie, as she sat on her mum's bed, waiting for her to get ready.

She took out her phone and tapped *Kestrel Island* into Google. As she scrolled through the photos of the beautiful landscape she could see why the campaigners felt so strongly about their cause.

'Wow,' she said. 'It looks so overgrown and natural. The family who used to own the island just let it grow wild. And look at this. There are deer living there and most of them have never even set eyes on people. They can't possibly allow someone to ruin all this.'

When they arrived at the library the meeting had already started. It was being held in a large room with a high ceiling and a small stage at one end. All the seats were taken and a lot of people were already standing, so they slipped in as quietly as they could and stood by a wall at the back.

At the other end of the room, a woman was on her feet. She was talking passionately about the rare butterflies and wildflowers that had disappeared on the mainland but still flourish abundantly on the island. Sophie really liked her enthusiasm.

Mike Tindall was seated to the woman's right. When he noticed Mrs Watson and Sophie enter the room he smiled at them and nodded. Then he joined in the applause as the woman finished speaking and got to his feet to address the crowd.

'Before we continue,' he said, 'I'd like to welcome two guests to our meeting this evening, Michelle Watson and her daughter Sophie.' He raised his hand and gestured towards the back of the room.

Everyone turned their heads to look at the two strangers who were standing against the wall. Sophie wasn't used to this sort of attention and she could feel her face reddening as she tried to smile.

'As some of you are probably aware,' Mike continued, 'Michelle is the Green Party spokesperson on local government. And as we have an important meeting with Dorset County Council later this week, I'm sure we'd welcome any advice Michelle could give us on how to get the council onto our side.'

'Put all your plastic bottles in the green box!' shouted Mrs Watson, which was greeted with laughter and a small smattering of applause. Sophie knew a good joke when she heard it. She joined in the applause and gave her mum a big smile.

When the laughter had died down an elderly man in the front row stood up.

'One thing I'd like you to ask the council,' he said, 'is why they've let these people build on Kestrel Island in the first place. There's plenty of unoccupied warehouse space on the outskirts of town. Why do they need to spoil this beautiful island? And why are these people being so secretive? Perhaps they've got something to hide.'

'Yes,' said a woman over to the left. 'We've seen a lot of boxes with Hazardous Chemical stickers on them being loaded onto their speedboat down at the harbour.

There are rumours going around the town they're trying to develop some sort of chemical plant.'

'What are we going to do about it then?' shouted a man sitting three rows back. It was the first time Mike had seen him at any of the meetings and at first he was a little taken aback. He was a tall man, a little overweight, with a shaved head and small tattoos of a scorpion on either side of his neck. He leaned back in his chair with his arms folded waiting for Mike to respond.

'Well,' said Mike, 'we have a protest organised for tomorrow morning outside the town hall. And then later in the week, we're going to Dorchester to present a petition of ten thousand signatures to the planning department of the county council.'

'Yeah, and they'll just use that as scrap paper!' shouted the man. 'Or they'll listen politely and once you've gone they'll put your petition in the shredder.'

He stood up and turned to address the crowd.

'All these meetings and petitions don't mean anything!' he shouted. 'What we need is a bit of direct action. We should go to the island and confront these people. Get a small flotilla of boats. Video what they do to us on our phones. OK, there might be a few casualties but they can't stop all of us.'

Everyone in the room just sat and looked at him. This was not what they got involved in the protest movement for. They favoured peaceful demonstration and letters to the council, not taking on an army of security guards.

'Yes, thank you for that,' said Mike. 'I don't really think that's what this movement is all about.'

'Well, in that case, you're doing exactly what the people on the island want you to do,' said the man. 'You're behaving yourselves, like a bunch of liberal do-gooders, while they just carry on doing exactly what they want.'

He pushed his way to the side of the room, stepping on a few feet as he did. Then he stormed angrily out, barging into Sophie as he passed her. She thought he smelled of alcohol and armpits. It took a while to get the odour out of her nostrils.

Once he'd gone there was an uneasy quiet for a few seconds. The earlier mood of optimism had been well and truly punctured.

After the meeting was over Sophie and her mum waited around to see if they could have a word with Mike.

'That man who got angry did have a point,' said Mrs

Watson, when they finally had a chance to talk to him. 'They may be polite when you first present the petition to the council, but once you've left they'll probably just file it away.'

'I know this is a bit of a cheek,' said Mike, 'but I don't suppose you'd come with us when we meet with the council later in the week? It would really strengthen our case to have the party's local government spokesperson involved in our campaign. You'd be very welcome too, Sophie.'

'I'd be happy to, if you think it would help,' said Mrs Watson. 'What do you think Sophie? Fancy a trip to Dorchester?'

CHAPTER 8

The following day at breakfast, Mrs Watson was bubbling with excitement about the protest that was planned for that morning.

'Mike's done such a good job organising the opposition to this development,' she said, 'and he seems to have done it all on his own. I hope you don't mind me offering to help out?'

'Not at all,' said Sophie, 'and count me in as well. I can't believe the council have allowed this development to go ahead. Surely they could have found somewhere more suitable on the mainland.'

'Quite right,' said Mrs Watson. 'As someone said at the meeting last night, these people must have something to hide. Nobody is allowed to visit the island and they refuse to say what they're developing. Why all the secrecy?'

Sophie looked across the room and saw Sienna standing in the doorway. They smiled at one another.

'There's your friend Sienna,' said Mrs Watson. 'Shall we ask her if she'd like to join us? It's no fun eating breakfast on your own.'

Sienna was happy to accept their invitation. And as the three of them ate breakfast together the conversation didn't stray far from the events surrounding Kestrel Island. Mrs Watson had become a bit obsessed with the protest, and Sophie and Sienna were happy to steer the talk away from anything connected to Sienna's background.

'So what are your plans for today Sienna?' said Mrs Watson eventually. 'Do you have anything exciting on the agenda?'

'Well, I was hoping to have a look around the town this morning,' said Sienna, 'just to get my bearings.'

'If you'd like some company I'd be happy to look around the town with you?' said Sophie. 'The protest should be finished by twelve thirty. We could have a wander around after that.'

'Thank you,' said Sienna. 'That would be nice.'

'You're welcome to join us at the town hall as well,' said Mrs Watson. 'After all, it's the future of your planet they're trying to protect.'

Sophie and Sienna glanced at one another but said nothing.

The protest outside the town hall was due to start at eleven thirty, so they met Sienna in the lobby at eleven fifteen and strolled through the town together enjoying the morning sunshine. The local newspapers had been invited to cover the event, and Mike Tindall was even hoping that TV and radio reporters might turn up.

When they arrived at the town hall, they were surprised by the carnival atmosphere the protest was generating. The crowd seemed to number three or four hundred and there was an abundance of placards with slogans like 'No Development on Kestrel Island' or 'Just Say No'. Two of the protesters, who were dressed up in bird costumes, were carrying placards saying 'Hands off Our Nesting Sites'. A group of children were dressed as butterflies and held up banners saying 'Help! We're Disappearing'. There were whistles and bells and a large jolly man was banging on a bass drum to orchestrate the chanting. Another group of people were wearing dust masks and carrying placards that said 'We Don't Want Your Chemical Plant'. It was noisy and good natured and everyone seemed to be having a good time. Mike

Tindall was on the steps of the town hall holding a megaphone. It looked like he would be making a speech at any minute.

Over to one side, two policemen were keeping an eye on proceedings. They seemed to know some of the protesters and were happy to share a joke with them from time to time. Further up the High Street, a police transit van was parked with more police sitting patiently inside. Behind it was a dog handler van.

'It's a great turn out isn't it?' said Mrs Watson.

She spotted Mike on the other side of the road and waved to him, but in the hubbub he didn't notice her.

'I'm just going to let Mike know we're here,' she said. 'See if there's anything we can do to help.'

She disappeared into the crowd, dodging placards and smiling at everyone she passed.

Shortly after eleven thirty, the doors of The White Lion opened and Sophie noticed the shaven-headed man from last night's meeting emerge.

'There's that man from last night,' she said. 'I didn't think he'd be turning up. He said these protests were a waste of time.'

He had several friends with him this time, and as the protest continued they mingled with the crowd and started joining in the chanting. They seemed so out of place with the rest of the mild-mannered activists that some of the protesters were clearly intimidated by the aggression they were displaying. Soon they were starting to orchestrate the chanting themselves.

'We want to go to Kestrel Island!' they chanted repeatedly.

Within a few minutes, the protest was joined by another large group of aggressive looking young men who appeared suddenly from East Street. They seemed to know the shaven-headed man and his friends and they joined in the chanting, enthusiastically ramping up the noise. Their actions were generating an intimidating atmosphere and Mike and some of the protesters were looking quite concerned.

Sophie was also starting to feel a little uncomfortable. She wasn't used to this level of hostility. She moved a little further away from the protest.

'I don't like the look of this,' she said. 'Why are they being so disruptive?'

The next few events happened so quickly that everyone was taken by surprise. A brick hit one of the windows of the town hall, then another. As the crowd surged back in panic they knocked an old lady to the floor and, in the confusion that followed, several people fell on top of her. When a policeman tried to help her up he was barged and jostled and someone landed a punch to the side of his head.

The police transit van was empty in seconds and the dog handlers were immediately on the scene. Scuffles had broken out between the protesters and the shaven-headed man's friends and several people were bleeding from cuts to the head. The High Street was now the scene of a full scale riot.

One of the aggressive young men clattered backwards into Sophie and Sienna, then turned and angrily shouted abuse at them. Sophie recoiled in horror, but Sienna just caught him by the hem of his jacket and threw him across the road into the gutter. He leapt to his feet instinctively, ready to do battle, but hesitated for a moment and then thought better of it. Sophie could understand why. Sienna emanated a raw power. She stood unblinkingly staring at the man, who backed off and disappeared into the crowd.

Mike Tindall was desperately trying to restore calm. He rushed down from the steps and started pulling people away from the trouble.

'Stop!' he shouted. 'This is a peaceful protest.'

But his pleas were largely ignored as the shaven-headed man and his friends were now running pitch battles with the police. Some of the protesters had ducked into a coffee shop to take cover and Sophie noticed Mrs Watson had joined them.

'Let's go and stand with Mum,' she said. 'Look, she's over there in the coffee shop.'

They rushed across the road trying to keep out of the rioters' line of fire and only just managed to get through the door before the staff locked it for their own safety.

'This is a disaster,' said Mrs Watson. 'The local papers are going to have a field day.'

The sound of police sirens signalled that re-enforcements were on the way and, as if working to a pre-arranged cue, the shaven-headed man and his friends suddenly drew back and melted into the surrounding streets. When order had finally been restored, the ground outside the town hall resembled the aftermath of a battlefield. It was covered in broken banners and several people were in need of medical treatment. Mike Tindall wandered amongst the debris shaking his head in shock.

Further down the road, a man with dark glasses was standing in a doorway. Sophie recognised him immediately. It was the mystery stranger who had been photographing the protesters yesterday. He lifted up his phone and took a few photographs then slipped it back in his pocket.

Sophie turned to Sienna and her mum.

'Do you see that man in the doorway on the other side of the street?' she said.

'What man?' said Mrs Watson.

'That man….'

But when she looked back, he had gone.

CHAPTER 9

Twenty minutes later, Sophie and Sienna were sitting in a cafe in East Street talking over the events they had just witnessed.

'Well, I wasn't expecting that,' said Sophie, still a little shaken from the experience. 'One minute there was a party atmosphere and the next it turned into a riot.'

'Yes, it was a bit strange wasn't it?' said Sienna. 'Those men who arrived looked as though they were carrying out a well-planned mission.'

'Do you think someone put them up to it?' said Sophie. 'The man who was at the library last night was just as hostile there, and Mike told Mum he'd never actually seen him before.'

Sophie waited for a response from Sienna but none was forthcoming. Instead, Sienna had her hands over her face and was peeking out through the gaps between her fingers.

'Don't turn around,' she said, 'but there's a car parked across the road with two men sitting in it, and I'm sure one of them is Osorio.'

'Osorio?' said Sophie. 'Isn't he the man you're looking for?'

'Yes. I'm going to keep my head down and cover my face so you can turn and look.'

When Sophie turned to look at the car there was a surprise for her as well. It was the black car that almost ran Sophie and her mum off the road earlier in the week. The person in the driving seat was the same man who had driven so recklessly. It was Rupert Flynn. So the man in the passenger seat must be Osorio.

Sophie studied him for a few seconds aware that, just like Sienna, he wasn't from this world. He had dark hair drawn back from his face and the paleness of his skin was made more apparent by his dark goatee beard. He sat impassively looking straight ahead.

'If that is Osorio he seems to have found a friend in town,' said Sophie. 'The man who's driving the car is Rupert Flynn. He's the person all these protests are about.'

Sienna moved her chair to the side of the table so she was partially concealed behind a pillar.

'I wonder what Osorio wants with Mr Flynn,' she said.

'Well, from what I've heard, if he was looking to make contact with pure evil he's found the person he's been looking for.'

Sienna continued to watch the car as Flynn talked on the phone in an aggressive manner. He paused for a moment and consulted with Osorio, then carried on ranting at whoever was on the other end of the phone. When the call finished he slipped the phone back in his pocket, then pulled the car out into the traffic and drove away. The girls sat in silence for a few moments. Sienna seemed to be deep in thought.

'It's a weird coincidence that both you and Osorio should end up in Bramlington Bay,' said Sophie eventually.

'It's not that much of a coincidence,' said Sienna. 'There are only a few points on the earth where it's possible to transfer between worlds and the coastline in this area is one of them. Osorio has been known to use this portal before, so my father suggested I start looking here.'

'Well, it hasn't taken you long to find him has it?' said Sophie.

'No, it hasn't, but that doesn't surprise me either. Osorio has visited your world many times and we know he's quite familiar with this area. He has contacts and associates in this town, and he's arrogant enough to believe he can stay safely hidden here.'

They paused in their conversation for a moment when the waiter arrived with the drinks. When they were able to speak freely again, Sophie listened intently as Sienna talked of the man she had come to earth to find.

'Osorio was once a young and idealistic Senator,' she said, 'keen to build a bright future for his people. But as he attained more power he became disillusioned with the Senate, believing they lacked ambition. He wanted us to build a mighty empire by exploring, invading and colonising other worlds. He realised he had no support within the Senate, so he sought the help of less democratic forces, promising them great power and influence. When they tried to seize power in a military coup, many of the armed forces remained loyal to the government and the coup failed. Osorio must have realised all was lost. He fled from the Senate, taking The Orb with him, and has been hiding out in this world ever since.'

'What do you think his plans are now?' Sophie asked.

'He's probably trying to build support for another attempt to seize power. His plan may have failed but he'll try to persuade others to join the cause.'

'Well, it looks like Flynn's impressed already,' said Sophie.

'I have to find out what they're doing on Kestrel Island,' said Sienna. 'If Osorio is involved they'll definitely have to be stopped.'

'You're not thinking of going there are you?' said Sophie.

'Well, I don't think he's going to come to me, so it looks like I'll have to go looking for him,' Sienna answered. 'Only by being in possession of The Orb for a significant period of time will Osorio see any benefit. Therefore, the quicker I can get to him the less chance there is of him making use of it. If I can take it from him, even for a few moments, the benefit he has already gained will be lost and he'll have to start again.'

'But Mike says the guards who are patrolling the island have been roughing people up if they trespass. What if you get hurt?'

'What if I don't?' said Sienna. 'What if I find Osorio and get The Orb back?'

'But there are lots of them and you're …..well…'

'I'm a girl? Is that what you mean?' Sienna snapped.

'No,' said Sophie. 'Well, sort of no. I mean Flynn and Osorio both sound like maniacs. Why would you put yourself in that sort of danger?'

'Because it's the right thing to do,' said Sienna. 'I'm not going to pretend I'm not scared - I am scared - but I'm not going to let that put me off. And besides, I don't really have any choice. Until I regain possession of The Orb I can't return to my home.'

If this had happened in one of Sophie's favourite books she would have found it tremendously noble and exciting. But she was starting to grow fond of Sienna, and she was worried that her new friend was taking too big a risk. She had to find a way of making her see sense.

CHAPTER 10

The trip to Dorchester meant the first early start of the holiday. The meeting with the council was scheduled for ten o'clock so Mike had arranged to pick Sophie and her mum up at nine.

When Sophie drew back the curtains to let in the outside world the sky was overcast and grey. Spits and spots of rain peppered against the window, driven by the offshore wind that often battered the town.

Out at sea, she spotted a sailing boat being tossed about on the waves like a feather. Some brave soul who would rather try to harness the power of the elements than plump for the safety of harbour. Sophie couldn't see the attraction of being out on a day like today. She felt cosy and reassured to be safe inside in such dreadful weather.

Mike arrived in the lobby just before nine, limping

slightly and looking battered and beaten up. His lip was swollen and badly cut and a large bruise had developed on the right hand side of his face. He tried not to notice the look of horror on the faces of Sophie and her mum as he greeted them.

'Mike. What happened?' said Mrs Watson. 'You look terrible.'

'I bumped into Mr Flynn yesterday afternoon,' said Mike, 'and we didn't see eye to eye.'

'Did he attack you?' Sophie asked.

'Well, sort of. We got into a fight.'

Sophie and her mum gasped.

'After the riot at yesterday's protest,' Mike continued, 'I went to the local newspaper office to try to convince their reporter that we're not a bunch of thugs and hooligans. But as I left the building Rupert Flynn was standing directly outside the door. We had a frank exchange of views and it quickly escalated into a fight. I just hope we weren't spotted by any photographers, or their front page next Friday could be me and Flynn rolling around on the floor trading punches.'

'Rolling around on the floor?' said Mrs Watson, incredulously.

'I'm afraid so,' said Mike. 'It all got a bit out of hand.

Flynn stormed off making the usual angry threats. Told me I'm a dead man walking. But he'll be even angrier when he looks in the mirror this morning. I'm sure he doesn't look any better than I do.'

'Shouldn't you be careful how you deal with Mr Flynn?' said Sophie. 'Uncle John said people who get in his way often end up having accidents.'

'I'm not going to let him scare me off,' said Mike. 'My dad always told me you should stand up to a bully, and that's exactly what Flynn is.'

As they left the hotel it was starting to rain quite heavily. They buttoned up their jackets, turned their collars up and made a run for the car. The rain was coming down hard as they drove through the town. It bounced off the pavement and fast moving streams ran along the gutters and raced down the hill in torrents.

By the time they reached the narrow country roads that would take them up to the main road to Dorchester, thunder was rumbling overhead. It was a good thing Mike was so familiar with the roads they were using. The rain was now torrential and at regular intervals the car crashed through an enormous puddle. Some of them were so deep they smacked against the underside of the car, drenching the hedges on either side with spray. The windscreen wipers were clearing the rain as fast as they could, but at times it was difficult to see very far ahead.

'I don't know why big trucks are allowed to use these little country lanes,' said Mike, looking in his rear view mirror. 'That idiot behind me is driving so close that if I had to stop suddenly he'd have no time to react.'

Sophie turned around to look at the truck. It was so close it gave her the feeling that it was looming over them, blocking out the light. It took up almost the whole of the road. Suddenly they felt the truck shunt into the back of them.

'What the....?' said Mike, trying to steady the car on the slippery surface.

He leaned on the horn and turned on his hazard lights in an effort to get the truck to back off. But it did the complete opposite. It shunted them again, and then again. Each time it hit them Sophie was jolted out of her seat.

'What's happening?' she shouted.

'I think it's deliberately ramming us!' Mike replied, trying desperately to keep control of the car.

He accelerated to try to shake the truck off, but the driver seemed determined that wasn't going to happen. It kept pace with them relentlessly and was never more than a few feet from their bumper. The road was twisting and turning and in the atrocious weather Mike was struggling to hold the car onto the road. There was nowhere to turn off and nowhere to stop as the truck kept battering them repeatedly.

'Why are they doing this?' Sophie shouted, gripping the seat with both hands.

They heard something pop and instantly one of the wing mirrors shattered.

'Oh no, now I think they're shooting at us!' Mike shouted.

'Get down in your seat, Sophie!' shouted Mrs Watson. 'Keep your head down!'

They heard two more pops and something hit the front of the car, then another pop and a bang as one of the front tyres blew out. They were now travelling so fast that Mike couldn't keep control of the car as it weaved alarmingly from side to side. Instinctively, he slammed his foot on the brake, but that just made matters worse, sending the car into a spin. It crashed sideways into a tree, showering them with fragments of glass, then rolled over several times, bounced along a fallow field and ended up in a ditch.

For a few seconds everything was still. Then Sophie

put her hand up to her face. She could feel warm liquid on the side of her head. She looked at her hand. It was smeared with blood. Fighting back the urge to throw up, she took a deep breath to steady herself. Then she saw her mum's head lolling against the window of the door.

'Mum!' she shouted, leaning forward between the two front seats.

Mrs Watson and Mike both looked to be unconscious, but they did seem to be breathing and at least the car had landed the right way up. She pushed the door open and got out into the muddy field. The rain was now coming down so hard it was battering against her head and shoulders, washing the blood off her face and hand. A flash of lightning lit up the area spookily, closely followed by a deafening crash of thunder.

There was nobody else around and the truck had disappeared. She inched the front door open and eased her mother back into her seat.

'Mum!' said Sophie frantically. 'Are you OK?'

Mrs Watson stirred but didn't answer. At least she was conscious. Mike looked to be in a much worse condition though. He was bleeding heavily from a cut to the head and covered with shards of glass from the shattered windscreen.

She got back into the car, pulled out her phone and punched in 999. When a voice answered she spoke without waiting.

'There's been an accident. We need an ambulance!' she shouted. 'And the police. Someone's been shooting at us!'

'OK, madam,' said the woman at the other end of the phone. 'Could you tell me exactly where you are?'

'Erm…. I'm not sure,' said Sophie. 'We were driving to Dorchester from Bramlington Bay when someone in a truck started shooting at us. My mum and Mr Tindall are badly injured. They need an ambulance urgently.'

When Sophie was put through to the ambulance service they asked her the same questions and she gave the same answers.

'There's no time for all this!' Sophie shouted. 'Send an ambulance, please!'

'Someone is on their way to you as we speak,' said the operator, 'but I need to ask a few more questions while you wait for them.'

Within five minutes Sophie could see a helicopter approaching in the distance. When it reached the field where the car had ended up it circled for a while, then hovered high above Sophie's head, its lights blinking against the dark sky. A few minutes later she heard the sound of sirens and, seconds later, two ambulances and a police car were on the scene. The medics ran across the muddy field towards the car, stumbling occasionally on the uneven ground. Sophie watched nervously as they ran through their emergency procedures then lifted Mrs Watson and Mike onto stretchers.

While the ambulances sped through the traffic towards the local hospital Sophie held her mum's hand praying that she would be alright. Looking at her mum's face made the harsh reality of what had just happened begin to sink in. Someone had tried to kill them. And by blowing out one of Mike's tyres they'd managed to make it look as if it was an unfortunate accident in terrible weather. Whoever did this mustn't be allowed to get away with it.

CHAPTER 11

Sophie didn't say much when John arrived at Dorset County Hospital. She was still coming to terms with what had happened. Sitting by the side of the bed holding her mum's hand, she smiled briefly when he first appeared.

'They've given her something to help her sleep,' she said. 'It looks like they'll be keeping her in for a few days while they run some tests. And I tried to phone Dad but I think he must have his phone switched off.'

'Don't worry about your dad,' said John, 'I've just had a chat with him. He's going to come down tomorrow. And I've spoken to the doctor as well. They're only keeping your mum in as a precaution. It's nothing to worry about.'

'Did the doctor say how Mike's doing?' Sophie asked.

'The only thing they've told me is that he's got a bad head injury.'

'Yes, it looked quite serious when they were getting him out of the car,' she said.

As she changed into the clean clothes John had brought her from the hotel, Sophie looked in the bathroom mirror at the cut to the side of her head. The doctor said she'd been lucky, it didn't even need stitches.

John took the long way round as they travelled back to Bramlington Bay, to avoid using the road where the accident had occurred. Sophie was unusually quiet, watching the road constantly and occasionally looking around to see who was behind them.

'It wasn't an accident you know,' she said, after a long silence.

'Did you tell the police that?' John asked.

'Yes, I did. They said they're having the car towed back this afternoon and their forensic team will be compiling a full report. They were a bit surprised when I said we'd been shot at, but hopefully they'll find some evidence of that when they inspect the car.'

'Did you get a look at who was driving the truck?'

'No, they were too close to us, and to be honest it was such a frightening experience that never really occurred to me.'

'Of course not,' said John.

'We all know who was responsible though don't we?' she said.

'Who's that?'

'Rupert Flynn,' said Sophie. 'Mike got involved in a fight with him yesterday and afterwards Flynn threatened to kill him.'

'Yes, but Flynn's threatened to kill half the people in the town at one time or another,' said John.

'But Mike's the person who's trying to stop him from building on Kestrel Island. You said the other day that people who get in Flynn's way tend to end up having accidents.'

They drove in silence for a few more minutes with Sophie staring blankly at the road ahead.

'Why all this fuss over a stupid island?' she suddenly snapped.

'Well,' said John, 'people in the town feel quite strongly.......'

'Yes, but it's not worth dying for is it?' she shouted. 'My mum's lying in a hospital bed just because some lunatic wants to get his own way.'

'Your mum's going to be OK,' said John.

'But she shouldn't be there at all,' Sophie shouted angrily. 'The people of this town should have dealt with

Flynn a long time ago. I'll tell you, if anything happens to Mum...... I'll kill him. I'll kill him myself.'

Something was stirring inside Sophie, something that had lain dormant for many years. The part of her that believed in natural justice, integrity and truth was rising up and demanding attention. In her comfortable and gentile existence living in Hampton Spa, she was protected from the harsher realities of life. Whatever difficulties she encountered it was usually possible for her to find an amicable solution. But she and her mum could have died that morning and somehow she knew that this time she couldn't just look the other way. It was time to stand up for the things that really mattered.

When she got back to the hotel Sophie went up to her room and phoned her dad. It was comforting to hear his voice. He told her he'd had a long talk with the doctors and had been reassured that there was nothing to worry about.

'They told me to phone later this afternoon,' he said. 'She should be awake by then. I was going to jump in the car and come straight down but I thought I'd better speak to your mum first. You know what she's like? She thinks I fuss too much.'

'I've really missed you, Dad,' said Sophie.

'I've missed you too darling. And I'm so glad that you're OK.'

The rain of the morning slowly cleared away and was followed by a warm and sunny afternoon. As Sophie passed through the lobby on her way out to the garden the daily papers were spread out on a table for the guests to help themselves. All the front pages carried photographs of the missing scientist Julius Merrick. Sophie stopped and studied his face. She thought he looked like a kind man and bore a striking resemblance to Bill Gates. There were also photos of his tearful daughters appealing for information on his whereabouts. They looked heartbroken. With her mum lying injured in a hospital bed Sophie could really feel their pain.

Sitting in the garden on the bench under the willow tree she gathered her thoughts and tried to make sense of everything that had happened. She and her mum had survived an attempt to kill them, and Mike was still seriously injured. It was a terrifying experience. She could still picture the truck looming over them menacingly and her panic as the car skidded off the road. The thought of her mum being carried to an ambulance in the pouring rain brought tears to her eyes.

She took out her phone and called the hospital to find out if there was any news. To her delight, Mrs Watson was awake and in good spirits. They chatted for about twenty minutes about this and that and Sophie promised to visit the following morning.

'You just concentrate on getting better,' she told her mum. 'We've still got a holiday to enjoy.'

Just as she hung up, the door at the back of the hotel opened and Sienna stepped out onto the patio. She noticed Sophie sitting in the shade and walked across the grass to join her.

'John just told me what happened this morning,' she said. 'Are you OK?'

'I think so,' said Sophie. 'I'm not injured anyway, apart from this cut on my head.'

'And how are you feeling?'

'That's what's weird,' said Sophie. 'I'm not sure how I feel. I mean, I'm angry and a bit jangled, but I….. I don't know…'

'You don't know what to do about it?' Sienna suggested.

'Yes, maybe that's it. Most of the time my life is fairly easy going, and if things don't work out it doesn't really matter too much. But someone tried to kill us this morning.'

'And you want to get back at them?'

'Yes, I think I do,' said Sophie. 'When I was travelling back from the hospital I told Uncle John that if Rupert Flynn turned out to be responsible I'd kill him myself. I was a bit shocked to hear myself say that.'

'Do you think it was Flynn?'

'Well, he had a fight with Mike yesterday afternoon during which he told Mike he was a dead man walking. It's a bit of a coincidence that the following day someone tried to kill us.'

'I think we'll have to find out what Mr Flynn is up to,' said Sienna. 'If he's involved with Osorio a lot more people could end up getting hurt. John told me Flynn lives in The Manor House on the north side of the town. I'm going out there tonight to see what I can find out.'

'We can't just break into his house,' said Sophie. 'That would make us criminals as well.'

'I'm not necessarily going to break in,' said Sienna. 'I just want to have a look around to see if there's any sign of Osorio. And what do you mean *we* can't just break in?'

'I mean I'm going with you.'

'Are you sure about this Sophie? This doesn't sound like your kind of thing.'

'Dead sure,' said Sophie. 'If Flynn was responsible for what happened this morning I want to find some proof. Maybe then the police will believe this wasn't just an unfortunate accident.'

CHAPTER 12

The sun had already set when they left the hotel and started walking towards the north side of the town. It was a clear night. After the torrential rain earlier in the day, the air felt fresh and clean. The moon was almost full.

Up ahead they noticed a fox crossing the road. It paused and stared at them haughtily as if *they* were the intruders. Then it trotted into a garden and sniffed and scratched around a dustbin, wondering if it could find a way in.

Sophie could feel the nerves jangling in her stomach.

'I feel like I'm going on a commando expedition,' she said, in an effort to hide her fear.

'Well, we're definitely dressed for one,' Sienna answered, noticing the similarity in their clothing.

They were both dressed for action, wearing jeans, boots and a short jacket.

'Yes,' said Sophie. 'It looks like I'm on a late night hike with my big sister.'

'Do you have any brothers or sisters?' Sienna asked.

'No,' said Sophie. 'What about you?'

'None,' Sienna answered. 'To be honest, I think that was the main problem when I was growing up.'

'How do you mean?'

'Well, I think my father really wanted to have a son and when he ended up with just one daughter it was a bit of a disappointment to him. So I always felt I had to do better than any of the boys in our neighbourhood just to get his approval.'

'Wow,' said Sophie. 'That must have been tough. I'll bet he was really proud of you when you were offered a place at The Academy though.'

'Yes, I think that was the moment when everything was finally alright between us. I'd still like to have had some brothers or sisters though.'

'Well, you've got one tonight,' said Sophie. 'As you said earlier, this isn't normally my sort of thing, so looks like you're stuck with your little sister for the evening.'

Sienna smiled. She liked the idea of going on an adventure with her little sister.

The north side of the town was where the big houses

were situated. Each one was set back from the road, often hidden from the prying eyes of the outside world by tall trees or large fences. Electronic gates and CCTV systems were in evidence everywhere. This was where the people with money lived.

They left the main road and walked up the gravel track that led to the large wrought iron gates of The Manor House. The grounds were surrounded by a ten-foot-high wall and it seemed the only way in was through these massive metal gates.

'Oh no,' said Sophie. 'He couldn't make it easy could he?'

She knew this was the point of no return. Once they were inside the grounds there was no turning back.

Sienna looked at the gates. They could easily have climbed over them but that may have been a little reckless. Even though it was dark they needed to do this without drawing any attention to themselves.

'Let's circle around the wall and see if there's a chance to scale it at some point,' she said.

Trees and shrubs grew abundantly on both sides of the wall. It felt like they were walking through the local woods. It was deathly quiet. The light from the moon was just enough for them to see where they were going, but every step they took crunched and snapped in the still night air.

'What are you like at climbing trees?' said Sienna.

'I've never climbed a tree,' said Sophie. 'And that's probably the main reason I've never fallen out of a tree and injured myself.'

'Well, I think I've found a way in,' Sienna said.

She pointed at a large tree about twenty metres away.

'All we have to do is climb that tree over there until we reach the branch that stretches out over the wall…'

'Is that all?' said Sophie, sarcastically. She may have been smiling, but inside she was desperately trying to bury her simmering fear.

'Not quite. Then we scooch along the branch and drop onto the top of the wall.'

'And then what?' said Sophie. 'Finish on a song?'

'No,' said Sienna, smiling at her. 'We make our way along the top of the wall to that tree inside the grounds. The fat branch that hangs out over the wall should be able to hold our weight.'

'You haven't mistaken me for Spiderman, have you?'

'Who's Spiderman?' Sienna asked.

'He's someone who's a lot better at climbing than I am.'

When they reached the tree Sienna scaled the bark

like a squirrel. Then she gripped the large branch with her hands and legs and shuffled along it until she could easily drop onto the wall.

'The wall's quite wide,' she whispered. 'It's fairly easy to walk along.'

Sophie started to climb the tree. When she reached the branch that stretched out over the wall she was beginning to gain a bit of confidence. But as she reached out to grab the branch her foot slipped and her shin scraped across the jagged bark. She closed her eyes and winced with pain. Fortunately, she still had a firm grip on the branch. She steadied herself and looked down to where she might have fallen.

'Don't look down,' said Sienna, 'just keep climbing.'

Sophie leaned cautiously out and grabbed the branch with her other hand.

'Now grab the branch with your legs.'

She swung her legs up to grip the branch but missed and was left swinging from the branch fifteen feet in the air.

'Grab the branch with your legs,' said Sienna frantically.

Sophie tried again and this time she managed to get one of her legs around the branch, then the other. She clung on for dear life.

'Now make your way over here by moving your hands towards me, but keep holding on with your legs.'

Shuffling cautiously along the branch she eventually reached the wall. As she released the grip of her legs Sienna grabbed her around the waist and helped her lower herself down onto the wall.

'And that's all there is to it,' said Sophie, once she was safely on the wall. 'Would you like me to show you how to do that again?'

Sienna smiled and shook her head.

'Well, you can show me on that tree over there,' she said. 'We still have to get inside, remember?'

'I was afraid you were going to say that.'

As they inched their way along the top of the wall, Sophie felt very exposed. She could feel her legs starting to tremble but she wasn't sure whether it was because of all the physical exertion or just good old fashioned terror. The wall was quite thick but, with nothing to hold onto, she felt as if she could fall at any minute. When they finally arrived at the tree, Sienna reached out and grabbed the fat branch.

'Don't forget,' she said, 'it's hands first, then grip the branch with your legs.'

Within a few seconds she was sitting in the tree. Next

Sophie made her way across, a little more confidently this time, and soon they were both on the ground sheltering behind a large rhododendron bush.

'You're getting quite good at this,' said Sienna.

'Thanks,' said Sophie, 'but I'm much happier now I'm back on the ground.'

They crept through the shrubs and small trees that were scattered around the grounds until they were close enough to the house to work out a plan. There was a small section of evergreen hedge about thirty metres from the front door. They crouched down behind it and tried to keep themselves hidden.

Flynn may have had a repulsive personality, but his house was truly magnificent. The long gravel drive stretched up from the road and came to a rest in front of an exquisite Georgian villa. It was regal and elegant, in stark contrast to the obnoxious aggression of its owner. The frontage and the grounds were immaculately maintained and from what Sophie could see of the inside of the house it was furnished in a subtle and tasteful way.

'Wow,' she said. 'Nice house.'

A large van was parked on the expanse of gravel outside the front door. Some men were carrying boxes out of the house and loading them into the van.

'I wonder what they're up to,' said Sienna.

'Well, let's go inside and find out shall we?' said a voice from behind them.

They spun around. A security guard was standing behind them holding a gun.

'On your feet,' he said.

The girls stood up dejectedly. Sophie was now so far out of her comfort zone her fear was becoming overwhelming.

'Now put your hands behind your head and walk up towards the house,' he barked.

As he marched them up the gravel drive they were joined by another guard who was patrolling with two enormous dogs. They were both as big as a small pony and were straining on their metal leads. Sophie had a lifelong fear of dogs, and when she saw these two beasts she could feel her nerves jangling. She felt small and vulnerable and she could feel herself starting to shake. This was not how they'd intended the evening to go, but they would now have to face the reality of their failed plan. She and Sienna were trespassing and these people clearly meant business.

When they reached the house they could hear Rupert Flynn shouting at the men who were carrying boxes onto the van. He was holding a sheet of paper and ticking off the boxes as they were carried out of the house. His left eye was bruised and slightly swollen and there was a nasty graze on his chin. The suit he was wearing looked as if he'd slept in it.

'Get this lot down to Eastern Quay,' he bellowed, 'the boat will be there just after midnight. And tell the crew to wait for the car to arrive. We've got a passenger for them.'

He turned and saw the girls and their captors.

'Who the hell are these two?' he shouted.

'I found them hiding in the bushes over there, Mr Flynn,' said the security guard. 'They were spying on the house.'

Flynn looked at Sienna and narrowed his eyes.

'I know you from somewhere, don't I?'

Sienna just stared at him and said nothing.

Flynn looked at her a little while longer, deep in thought.

There was some movement over to their left. Sophie noticed another man standing in the doorway. He was tall and thin and had a dark goatee beard. He stared at Sienna intensely, his dark penetrating eyes filled with menace.

'So, your father is so weak he decided to send a girl after me,' he said.

Sienna inhaled sharply. It was Osorio, the man she had been hunting for.

'My father isn't weak,' she said, turning to face Osorio. 'And he didn't send me after you either. I am a member of The Elite, and I have come here to take The Orb back to its rightful place.'

Osorio burst out laughing.

'But you're just a girl,' he said. 'Are we filling our security services with children now?'

Sophie could see the anger rising up in Sienna.

'Your father is weak,' Osorio continued, 'too weak to use the power of The Orb. This power should be in the hands of someone who is brave and ambitious, that's what power is for.'

'You're the one who is weak Osorio,' said Sienna, through gritted teeth. 'That's why you feel you need The Orb. True power is in the heart and in the mind.'

'You foolish girl,' said Osorio, smiling menacingly at her. 'You still believe all that nonsense our elders have been preaching for generations. They tell us such things to keep us in our place. Your father has always been a weak man and he will cry like a baby when he hears the fate of his only daughter.'

'What happened to you, Osorio?' Sienna asked. 'You were once my father's friend.'

'That was a long time ago when your father was hungry and ambitious. Now he is feeble and complacent. I'll be doing him a favour by finishing his life.'

'He's twice the man you are and you know it,' Sienna shouted. 'That's why you're hiding out in this world like a frightened rabbit down a hole.'

The smile had now disappeared from Osorio's face. He turned angrily to the security guard who was standing by the door.

'Take them down to the cellar until we're finished here. Then drive them to Eastern Quay and put them on the boat out to the island. I have plans for the weakling's daughter.'

'OK, you two,' said the security guard, 'inside.'

They stepped into the large internal hallway.

'That small staircase over there!' shouted the guard. 'Move!'

Sophie and Sienna crossed the hall, made their way down the staircase and in through the door at the bottom. It was a completely enclosed cellar with no windows to the outside. A few old crates were scattered around at the far side of the room and a naked light bulb hung from the ceiling.

'Get over there by the wall,' said the security guard.

Once the girls were at the other side of the cellar he pulled the door shut, then locked and bolted it. Before going back upstairs he switched the light off from the outside and they were left in complete darkness.

They searched around with their hands and found two crates to sit on.

'Well, what do we do now?' said Sophie, struggling to stay composed.

'Try to find a way out,' said Sienna through the darkness.

CHAPTER 13

The cellar had a damp and musty smell. It was cold and clammy and Sophie found it unnerving having to sit in total darkness. But she was also glad that it was so dark. She didn't want Sienna to see the tears in her eyes. She couldn't believe they'd been caught so soon. Why had she been so determined to go with Sienna tonight? They may never get out of this alive. Flynn had already tried to kill her once and now she was locked in a pitch black cellar waiting to find out what else he had in store for her.

Something brushed against her face and she let out a yelp.

'What's the matter?' said Sienna.

'Something touched my face,' said Sophie. 'I think it might have been a spider's web.'

'I think spiders are the least of our problems,' said

Sienna. 'We've got to find a way out of here.'

But Sophie didn't see how they could possibly find a way out. Even if there was another door or window, it was so dark they'd be lucky to be able to find it.

'What are we going to do?' she said desperately. 'They're planning to take us out to the island. Then what? I don't want to die. This is all such a nightmare.'

She started to gently sob but felt a little comforted when Sienna's hand touched her on the shoulder.

'Nobody's going to die,' said Sienna, 'but we have to stay strong. The biggest weapon they have is our fear, but if we can stay calm and bide our time, eventually they'll slip up and give us a chance.'

'But they've got guns, and we already know Flynn is prepared to kill people to get his own way.'

'Yes, but we have to trust ourselves, Sophie,' said Sienna. 'We have to believe we can get out of this, otherwise we're allowing them to have all the power.'

They could hear people moving around upstairs, Flynn was shouting and doors were being slammed. Soon they heard some movement on the stairs and a key being turned in the lock. As the door swung open the light was switched on and, after such a long time in the dark, they were blinded by its intensity. Squinting and shielding their eyes from the light, they could just make out the silhouette of the security guard standing in the doorway.

'Right, up the stairs,' he said, pointing his gun towards the staircase. 'If you give me any trouble I'll make sure it's a slow and painful death. The choice is yours.'

When they reached the front door of the house, they could see the car carrying Flynn and Osorio passing through the metal gates at the end of the drive. The guard pointed towards a small van that was parked about thirty metres away.

'The van,' he said. 'Move!'

Sophie was feeling desperate. Then she remembered what Sienna had said about staying strong. She had to think of a plan. They couldn't let these people take them out to the island. The guard was a big man, but not very tall. Could they possibly overpower him? She knew Sienna was able to read her mind but she couldn't be sure Sienna was tuned in at that moment. But she decided to send her a message anyway. She was going to feign an ankle injury and throw herself onto the floor. It was a bit of a hare-brained scheme but it was all she could think of. As they approached the waiting van she knew it was now or never. She let out a yell and stumbled sideways, collapsing onto the grass in pain.

In the split second the guard's attention was distracted Sienna acted. Her first blow was to the man's windpipe. He let out a guttural sound and stumbled backwards gasping for air. He was so taken by surprise by the attack that he didn't see the second blow coming either, a ferocious punch to the side of the head that sent him clattering headfirst into the back of the van. He fell to the floor unconscious. Sienna immediately grabbed his gun and stuffed it into her back pocket.

'Help me drag him over there,' she said. 'We need to hide him behind those bushes in case one of the other guards comes along.'

The guard was quite heavy and it was hard going moving him. All the time they were dragging him Sophie kept looking around for the dogs, hoping desperately that they'd be sleeping at this time of night. When they reached the bushes, they rolled the guard out of sight then crouched down to catch their breath. Sophie could feel a cold sweat on her face.

Once it was clear there were no other guards around, the girls turned and walked quickly back through the trees, glancing back towards the house from time to time. Initially, everything was quiet apart from the sound of their footsteps. But before too long they heard the sound of a dog barking.

'Oh no,' said Sophie, 'please, not the dogs.'

There was a brief period of silence. Then they heard the dog barking again. Seconds later it seemed to be getting closer. Sophie panicked and started running. By now she wasn't really thinking clearly. Branches smacked against her face as she searched for the right direction but it was so dark she was like a rudderless ship. She smashed her shoulder against a large tree and stumbled to the ground. When she scrambled to her feet again, she had momentarily lost her bearings. Sienna dragged her out of the trees and they sprinted across the grass towards the wall.

By this point, Sophie was so afraid she was making no attempt to be quiet. Her only thought was to get to the other side of the wall as quickly as possible. Sienna was running alongside her urging her to keep going and not to look around. She didn't need to be told. The dog was now getting so close she could hear the sound of its paws pounding into the earth behind them. Her mouth was dry and tears were streaming down her face. Straining to get an extra bit of speed out of her legs, her heart was pounding in her chest and she was finding it hard to catch her breath.

When they reached the tree that would take them up to the wall, they both leapt onto it in desperation. Sienna was onto the higher branches in no time at all but Sophie took a second or two longer. Those extra seconds were just enough for the dog to reach them and catch Sophie by the foot. She could feel the power of its jaws as it gripped onto her boot. Its menacing growls were terrifying. Sienna reached down to try to grab hold of Sophie's arm but it was too late. The dog dragged Sophie from the tree and flipped her onto the grass like a rag doll. She could see its massive teeth and the saliva dripping from its jaws. It ran at her again in a crazed frenzy, intent on ravaging its prey.

But before it could get to her, Sophie heard the sound of a gunshot, and the dog staggered and fell to the ground. Sienna leapt from the tree brandishing the gun she'd taken from the guard and dragged Sophie back onto her feet again.

'Come on, we've got to get out of this place,' she said. 'That gunshot will have woken up everything within miles of here.'

She was right. Immediately they heard the sound of another dog barking and a man shouting at the top of the driveway. This time Sienna made sure Sophie went up the tree first, then she scrambled up after her, occasionally pushing her up to quicken their escape. By the time they were on the wall the other dog had almost reached them and one of the security guards wasn't far behind. Sophie felt so exposed on the top of the wall, like a tightrope walker between two tall buildings. If the security guard was any sort of a shot they would be such an easy target.

Finally, they reached the outside tree with the overhanging branch. As they did, a bullet hit the wall just below their feet. Instinctively, Sophie dived for the branch and hung on for dear life. She was aware that Sienna was still on the wall urging her to keep going.

Another shot rang out, this time it thudded against the trunk of the tree. Sienna crouched down low and fired off a series of shots. She saw the security guard dive for cover behind some low bushes and roll across the grass. Then she spun around and leapt for the branch, but in doing so she dropped her gun on the inside of the wall. Now they really did have to get away from there.

Sophie was already safely on the ground, and she watched in amazement as Sienna fairly flew across the branch using only her hands. It was both graceful and powerful. She didn't even seem to be breathing heavily.

They expected the roads around The Manor House to be swarming with security guards as they ran back towards the town, but none appeared. Whatever happened inside the grounds of The Manor House, Flynn must have wanted it to stay private. Even so, they kept on running. They'd already had one lucky escape. They didn't need another crisis.

CHAPTER 14

When they reached the town centre, they ducked into the bus station to take a desperately needed breather. It was bustling with energy as the late night revellers mingled with other weary travellers who were waiting for the last bus home.

Sophie was exhausted. Her legs were aching and her lungs were still desperately trying to take in enough air. She headed straight for the waiting area so she could find somewhere to sit down. It was a warm night and her clothes felt damp and sticky. She took off her jacket, slumped down into the seat and leaned back against the wall with her eyes closed.

'I think I must have run farther tonight than I have in the last year,' she said, still trying to catch her breath.

Sienna still looked quite fresh. She didn't even sit down.

'You don't normally do much running do you?' she said.

'No,' Sophie answered breathlessly. 'In Hampton Spa, we prefer to amble. It's an ambling kind of town.'

'Well, you were able to move at speed when that dog was after us. I was running as fast as I could and you were only just behind me.'

'It's amazing what you can do when you're terrified,' said Sophie, finally getting control of her breathing.

'It's amazing what you can do any time you challenge yourself,' said Sienna.

A late night kiosk was open selling soft drinks and snacks. They bought two bottles of water and drank them down thirstily.

'Did you pick up the message I was trying to send you as we walked towards that van?' Sophie asked.

'You bet I did,' said Sienna. 'You obviously didn't pick up mine though.'

'What message?' Sophie asked.

'I kept trying to tell you that I've got the message, now get on with it.'

'Oh,' said Sophie, 'sorry about that. You're pretty handy with your fists though, aren't you? Did you learn that at The Academy?'

'Yes, we trained every day in unarmed combat, but that's the first time I've ever had to use it.'

'Well, you certainly took that guard by surprise. I'll bet he won't be telling his friends he got the bruise on his face when he was beaten up by a girl.'

Sienna laughed. After the countless hours of training she'd put in she knew she was now a match for almost anyone. She was determined to make a success of this mission and make her father proud.

'We'd better get back to the hotel,' said Sophie. 'It won't be long before they decide to come looking for us.'

She took their empty bottles and threw them in the recycling bin.

'You know for someone who doesn't like to take too many risks you've had quite an eventful day,' said Sienna.

'I certainly have,' said Sophie. 'I'd never climbed a tree before, or been locked in a pitch black cellar. And I don't remember anyone ever trying to kill me either. So that's three more things I can cross off my bucket list.'

'Have you ever been to Eastern Quay?' Sienna asked.

'Why do you ask?'

'Because that's where the boat that was going to take

us to the island will be docking. Flynn told the driver to let the crew know they'd be having a passenger. And I think we can guess who that might be.'

'Who?'

'Osorio of course. If he gets onto that boat, then for the first time since I arrived I'll know exactly where he is.'

'And then what?' said Sophie.

'And then I'll go to Kestrel Island and get The Orb back.'

'Well, that all sounds quite simple. Nothing to it really, is there?'

'So, do you have any idea where Eastern Quay is?' Sienna asked.

'Not really,' said Sophie, 'but my guess is that it's towards the east.'

Sienna looked towards the heavens.

'Well, I've only been in your world a few days but even I could have worked that one out.'

'You're not thinking of going there now, are you? It's eleven thirty at night.'

'And the boat arrives just after midnight,' said Sienna. 'It would be madness if we didn't even go and take a look.'

'And what if there's no sign of Osorio?'

'In that case, I'll have to have a rethink.'

Sophie's heart sank. She knew what Sienna was saying made perfect sense but right now she just wanted to go back to the safety of the hotel. She'd had enough excitement for one night. She needed to hide and regroup. But there was also no way she was going to let Sienna go on her own. There was nothing else for it but to tag along.

They headed for the Tourist Information Office on the seafront where Sophie was sure they'd find some signposts to Eastern Quay. Sure enough, there was a detailed map on the outside of the building showing all the information they needed. Eastern Quay was only a ten minute walk away in the old part of the town, where the fishing vessels used to unload their catch ready to be taken up to market. Sophie and her mum had walked around it earlier in the week when they were exploring the town. The fishing fleet was now long gone. Private yachts and pleasure boats now jostled for space on the quay, while fish and chip shops and ice cream parlours provided welcome refreshments for the tourists.

They crept through the winding cobbled streets towards the quay. It was deathly quiet. In the houses they passed the lights were all out. People were already asleep, recharging themselves for the work of the following day. Bakers, postmen, teachers and businessmen, the working people who kept the engine of the town ticking over.

When they reached the main road that ran alongside the harbour, they could see some men loading boxes onto a boat. Flynn was standing on the quay shouting at them and occasionally waving his arms in a frantic manner. Sophie and Sienna ducked into a darkened doorway to keep themselves hidden, watching and waiting to see if Osorio appeared.

Once the boxes had been unloaded, the driver had a brief talk with Flynn then drove off towards the north of the town. There was still no sign of Osorio. Flynn was pacing up and down, occasionally looking at his watch.

'Where is he?' Sienna whispered. 'He's got to arrive soon, the boat looks as if it's ready to leave.'

Two things then occurred that made Sienna rethink what was happening. A car appeared at the far end of the harbour and started driving towards the boat.

'Here he is,' she whispered.

Flynn turned and shouted something towards the boat and suddenly Osorio appeared from below deck. He had been on the boat all along.

Sienna inhaled sharply.

'He's already on the boat,' she said. 'So who's in the car then?'

The car pulled up and the rear doors opened. Two men got out and walked over to Flynn. Sophie gasped when she saw the older man wearing a suit and tie. It was the missing scientist Julius Merrick. She recognised him immediately.

'That's Julius Merrick,' she whispered urgently.

'Who's Julius Merrick?' said Sienna.

'He's a famous scientist who has been missing for the last few days. It's been in all the papers.'

'Are you sure it's him?' Sienna asked.

'Yes, I'm sure. He's the spitting image of Bill Gates.'

'Who's Bill Gates?'

'He's a famous businessman,' said Sophie. 'He made a fortune out of computers.'

Merrick looked sullen and tired and appeared reluctant to get onto the boat. When Flynn tried to usher him forward Merrick pushed him away and there was an aggressive exchange of views. But in the end Merrick relented and he followed Flynn up the gangplank. As soon as they were all on board the engine started up. Then the boat moved slowly out into the open water and headed south towards Kestrel Island.

CHAPTER 15

It was a struggle getting out of bed the following morning. The muscles in Sophie's legs ached from the exertions of the previous night. She felt battered and bruised, and her shin had a nasty graze from her attempts to climb up the tree. As her mind re ran the pictures of last night's trip to The Manor House, she could feel her stomach starting to tense all over again. She could still vividly picture what it felt like when the dog had hold of her foot, and the terror she felt as she was dragged from the tree. If Sienna hadn't acted so decisively, she could have been ripped apart by that dog.

Her thoughts were abruptly cut short by the sound of someone banging on her bedroom door. She struggled out of bed and shuffled across the room to open it. Sienna was waiting impatiently outside.

'You're still in your nightclothes!' she said, sounding surprised.

'I was still in my bed a minute ago,' said Sophie sleepily.

Sienna marched into the room, clearly keen to get straight down to business.

'I've been thinking about that scientist we saw last night,' she said. 'Do you think he's involved in whatever Osorio and Flynn are up to? Maybe they're building a bomb or something.'

'I'm not sure he's that sort of scientist,' said Sophie. 'I think I heard on the news that he works in healthcare in some way. Let's Google him and find out.'

'Google him?' said Sienna. 'What does that mean?'

'I'll show you.'

She turned on her phone and tapped the name Julius Merrick into Google. The search results were dominated by the news about his disappearance but his Wikipedia page came up with the information they were looking for.

'Here it is,' said Sophie. 'He's devoted his career to developing drugs to help people with severe psychiatric conditions. Two years ago he and someone called Alexis Humbert were awarded the Nobel Prize for chemistry.'

'And I take it that's a good thing to win is it?' Sienna asked.

'It's probably the top award a scientist can win. It means he's the best in his field.'

'Well, I don't think they're developing a bomb then,' said Sienna. 'So why is he out there on the island?'

'I don't know. But I don't think it's a social event judging by the look on his face last night.'

'Yes, he didn't want to get on that boat did he?' said Sienna.

'You don't think they've kidnapped him do you?'

'Well, I'm going out there tonight so maybe I'm about to find out.'

'You're going out there?' said Sophie, visibly shocked. 'You can't Sienna. It's surrounded by guards. And we know from what happened last night that they're probably armed. They'll spot you coming a mile off.'

'Not if we go at night,' said Sienna.

'We?' said Sophie. 'Now hang on a minute. We only just got away with it last night. In fact, I've still got that dog's teeth marks on my boot. We could have been killed.'

'But we weren't. And because of that, we've become stronger.'

'I'm sorry Sienna. I'm not keen on putting myself

into that kind of danger again. Why don't we just tell the police what we know and let them deal with it?'

'Tell them what?' said Sienna

'That we know where Julius Merrick is. That it's possible he's being held against his will. Let them go over there and deal with it.'

'And then Osorio will disappear and I'll have to start all over again. I can understand why you might be reluctant to go with me, Sophie. This isn't your battle. But please give me one more night before you bring in the police. If I'm not back by tomorrow afternoon then you can tell them everything.'

Sophie threw her phone onto the bed and turned to Sienna.

'Don't you worry about dying?' she said.

'Why would I worry about that?' Sienna answered.

'Well, because you'll be massively outnumbered and Flynn is a murderous maniac.'

'But I can't go into this situation thinking I'm going to lose. If I did I'd just be beating myself before I'd even got started. I came here to get The Orb, and now I know where Osorio is I don't really have any choice but to go there and take it from him.'

'Please don't go Sienna,' said Sophie. 'Osorio knows

you're here now and we've already seen how Flynn deals with anyone who tries to stand up to him.'

Sienna sat for a moment, thinking about what she wanted to say.

'I know it looks like a terrible idea,' she said, 'but I've been waiting for an opportunity like this all my life. I'm the daughter of Memphis. I grew up knowing I had a famous father and I carried that burden into everything I did.'

'Why would having a famous dad be a problem?' said Sophie.

'Because everything I do is judged against his standards. To do quite well at something is regarded as a failure.'

'But that's so unfair.'

'Yes, that's what I thought when I was younger. I watched my friends doing reasonably well and saw their parents patting them on the back. But my father was never happy with anything other than excellence because that's what he had always demanded from himself.'

'I don't want to sound rude,' said Sophie, 'but he doesn't sound like he's much fun to be around.'

'I think he means well,' said Sienna. 'He's trying to help me in the only way he knows how. He just doesn't seem to realise I don't have the same hopes and dreams that he had. But by setting high standards he has given me one huge gift. The knowledge that it's my own responsibility to ensure I have a life that's worth living and that sometimes in life it's important to take a risk. When the odds seem insurmountable, it can make us feel very small and vulnerable. But there's a giant inside us all, and we can all be heroes. We just have to step out into the unknown and trust the strength that's inside us.'

She paused for a moment. She seemed to be dealing with the emotion that was welling up inside her. It took Sophie by surprise to see a chink of vulnerability in Sienna's steely exterior. She wanted to lean across and give her friend a cuddle but she wasn't sure how Sienna would respond.

'So you see I have to go to the island,' Sienna continued. 'This is my chance to step out of my fathers' shadow and stand alongside him as an equal. I'm not going to pretend I'm not scared, to be honest, I'm terrified. But sometimes you have to do the things that make you feel uncomfortable whether it puts you in danger or not. I'd hate to look back on this in years to come and realise that victory was close at hand but I was too scared to take on the challenge.'

Sophie was quite moved by Sienna's words. She'd never met anyone quite like her before, only read about them in the adventure novels she loved so much.

'You're like the Warrior Queen in an A. V. Simpson book,' she said.

Sienna laughed. It was a welcome relief to be able to let some emotion out.

'Maybe there's a Warrior Queen inside all of us,' she said, 'but as I grew up I've had to find mine a lot quicker.'

Sophie thought about how different her life was to Sienna's. She pictured her dad pottering around at home, checking and double checking whether the builders had turned off all their electrical equipment before they left. She loved him dearly, but she knew that if she didn't change the way she lived she was going to end up just like him.

'What time are you planning to leave?' she asked.

'Just after the sun goes down,' said Sienna.

'You'll need a boat to get to the island. And someone who knows how to handle it. And you'll definitely need the help of someone who worries constantly and thinks we'd have been better off staying on the mainland.'

'Do you have anyone in particular in mind?' Sienna asked, smiling at her.

'I'm sure I'll think of someone.'

When Sophie visited the hospital with John later that morning her mum was in quite a jolly mood.

'I spoke to your dad on the phone this morning,' she said. 'He can't come down until tomorrow because the builders haven't quite finished securing the house, but he said he should be here by early afternoon.'

'Oh, that's great,' said Sophie. 'It'll be so nice to see him. Any news about when they're going to let you out?'

'Possibly tomorrow but more likely the day after,' she answered. 'They're still waiting for the results of some of the tests I had.'

'What about Mike? Have they told you how he's doing?'

'I'm afraid he's going to be in for some time. But at least he's out of danger now, so that's something.'

They chatted for another hour or so, then Mrs Watson's lunch arrived and the nurse told them visiting hours were up.

'I'll phone you tomorrow morning Mum,' Sophie said, as she and John got up to leave.

The drive back to Bramlington Bay was a lot more jovial than it had been the last time they'd taken this journey. But John took the long way round once again, just to be on the safe side.

'Would you mind if I took your boat out this afternoon?' Sophie asked when they reached the outskirts of the town. 'It would be nice to get out onto the water again.'

'Not at all,' said John. 'It's not far from here, just past the Harbour Cafe. We can stop there before we go back to the hotel.'

When they reached the Harbour Cafe Sophie noticed a small jetty poking out into the sea. A series of small boats were tethered to it, all of them were of a similar size. John clambered down into a small sailing dinghy and unclipped the fastenings that held the cover in place, flipping off small pools of water from the overnight rain. Then he rolled back the cover to make space for Sophie to get on board.

'She's called Betsy,' he said. 'And she's a similar model to the one you learned to sail in. The only difference is there's an outboard motor on this one in case there's no wind.'

They spent about twenty minutes on the boat to give

Sophie a chance to familiarise herself with being on the water again. John showed her how the outboard motor worked. It all seemed fairly straightforward.

'I was thinking of taking Sienna out sailing this afternoon,' she said. 'I mentioned it to her this morning. She seemed quite keen.'

'Make sure you both wear life jackets,' he answered, smiling at her. 'Remember what happened the last time I went out sailing with her father.'

The girls had a fun afternoon sailing around the bay. There was very little talk of the challenge they would face that night. They sailed and chatted and laughed, and when the wind dropped towards the end of the afternoon Sophie started up the outboard motor and they chugged slowly back towards the jetty. It was a relaxed and happy interlude in stark contrast to the daunting challenge that lay ahead of them.

CHAPTER 16

Sienna untied the line that tethered them to the jetty and carefully climbed onto the boat. Once she was safely on board Sophie pushed Betsy away from their mooring and started up the outboard motor. She'd have preferred to cross the water without making quite so much noise, but it was a still and windless night so there was no point in putting up the sails.

They breathed in the salty air as the little boat bounced along on the waves, occasionally dousing them with a cooling spray. Up ahead they could see the outline of Kestrel Island silhouetted against the moon. Allowed to grow unfettered for several decades it was lush and covered in vegetation.

They knew that the south side of the island was quite rocky, with a few cliffs which faced out to sea, so they decided their best bet was to land the boat on the west side. It was the farthest point from the house and it gave them a good chance of arriving undetected. And according to the images they'd seen on the internet, it also had some small bushes and shrubs quite close to the beach where they could hide the little boat.

The journey took about fifteen minutes and the information they'd found on the internet turned out to be a great help. They carried Betsy up the beach and hid her in a small clump of bushes, then knelt down and gathered themselves for the task at hand. When Sienna's jacket fell open Sophie noticed she was carrying the knife with a carved handle carefully concealed in a shoulder holster. This wasn't just a spying mission. Sienna intended to take back The Orb no matter what.

The sight of the knife unnerved Sophie a little. She was hoping their mission would be more akin to burglary than all out war. In her mind, they were just returning something to its rightful owner, and if everything went to plan they'd be back in the boat before too long and heading back towards the mainland.

'It's a good thing it's a clear night,' she said. 'The light from the moon will make it easy for us to see where we're going.'

'Great,' said Sienna, 'but which way do we go?'

Sophie looked up at the sky for a few seconds.

'Well, there's Polaris, the north star, so it must be this way,' she said, pointing inland.

Sienna looked at her, clearly impressed.

'Where did you learn how to do that?'

'My dad taught me. He's got a telescope in the loft. We've spent hours up there together, just looking at the stars.'

'Sounds like fun,' said Sienna.

'Yeah, it is in the summer. But the rest of the year I'm happy to leave him to it.'

Sophie suddenly felt uncomfortable mentioning her close relationship with her dad. She knew Sienna's relationship with her own father was a sensitive issue, and she hoped she hadn't said anything to upset her.

'Come on, let's try to find that house,' she said, hoping to move on from the subject.

They moved inland a short distance, then slowly made their way east using the island's plentiful supply of shrubs and trees as cover. The smell of damp earth and rotting leaves now filled their nostrils, in stark contrast to the salty, fishy smell of the sea.

Sophie could feel her heart pounding away inside her chest at the thought of what lay ahead. But she kept reminding herself what Sienna had said to her that morning. Being scared doesn't have to stop you from doing the right thing. Yesterday someone tried to kill her mum and at that point, everything had changed for her.

Away from the coast the trees grew in abundance. There were large oak and beech trees which provided a host of potential nesting sites for the island's vast array of birds, and a variety of conifers whose seeds were an important food source for the local wildlife. From the mainland the island looked fairly flat but now that they were crossing it the reality was completely different. From time to time there were steep gradients and the girls had to watch their footing as the ground was still slippery from the morning's rain.

In a dense part of the woods, where the canopy of the trees blocked out the moonlight, it was suddenly pitch black. Something small and furry ran across their path and they both leapt back in alarm. Whatever it was, it quickly disappeared into the blackness.

Occasional flickers of light started to appear in the distance as they approached the house and soon they could make out the frame of the roof and a light on in one of the upstairs rooms. As the house had been built in a clearing in the forest, it was possible to get quite close without losing the cover of the trees. They crouched in the darkness, watching and listening. There didn't seem to be anyone around outside.

'Let's circle around to the other side of the house and see what we can find out,' said Sienna.

It was eerily quiet. Why were there no guards?

At the back of the house they saw an open window.

'There's our way in,' said Sienna.

Sophie inhaled sharply. She'd been OK up to this point but now it was starting to get really scary. They were at least thirty feet from the side of the house and they would be horribly exposed once they left the cover of the trees.

'I don't suppose there's a chance he'll just roll The Orb out to us then turn in for the night is there?' she said.

Sienna chuckled.

'We've come this far. There's no point in holding back now.'

Sophie took another deep breath.

'OK,' she said. 'Let's go.'

Sienna sprinted across the grass to the open window. She slipped quietly inside then beckoned for Sophie to follow. Sophie swallowed hard. This was a step into the unknown, and it wasn't something she was used to. She could feel herself trembling as she rushed across the open ground towards the window.

There wasn't much in the room apart from a large table that still contained the remnants of a meal that had been eaten earlier. Plates with bones that had been picked clean, some pathetic looking vegetables, and three empty glasses. In contrast to Flynn's house on the mainland, there wasn't much else in the room. The walls were bare and very little effort had been made on the decor. They crept across to the door. The house seemed very quiet.

Sienna pulled the door open a few inches and tentatively looked out. The only light in the hallway came from the upstairs landing. There didn't seem to be anyone around. They slipped out into the hallway and tried one of the other doors. It appeared to be a downstairs office. Once they were inside they silently closed the door again. This room was much busier, with a desk and chairs and a large filing cabinet. There was another smaller desk against the wall with an open laptop on it. A large map of Dorset was plastered to the wall. There were lots of papers strewn across the large desk. Sophie flashed the torch from her phone onto it and started examining some of the papers.

'Hey, look at this,' she whispered.

'What is it?' said Sienna.

'There are copies of magazine articles here claiming the government are trying to develop mind control drugs for the security services to use. And this one says that Nobel scientist Julius Merrick might be involved. So what's he doing here then?'

'And look at this,' said Sienna, rifling through a briefcase. 'A list of names. Who are these people?'

Sophie read through the list.

'John Murray, Digby Chance, Alison Chartwell. These people are all ministers in The British Government. What's this all about?'

Sienna grabbed the papers off the desk and put them in the briefcase with the list of names.

'We'll take these with us and work that out later,' she said. 'For now, let's concentrate on finding what we came for.'

Their focus was suddenly broken by the sound of someone shouting outside the house. Sophie froze. For a few moments she had allowed herself to believe that this would all be OK. Perhaps they could be in and out of the house without anyone noticing. But the sudden sound of voices had brought her back to reality and reawakened her fear. A light went on in the outside hallway. Someone had entered the house through the front door and was talking in a loud and aggressive voice. It was Rupert Flynn.

'Let's get out of here,' said Sienna.

She rushed to the window, unclipped the latch and opened it as quietly as she could. Sophie slipped out first, then Sienna. But as she dropped to the ground on the other side she clattered the briefcase against the window ledge and shattered the silence.

'What the hell was that?' she heard Flynn shout.

CHAPTER 17

The girls ran full pelt from the house. As they fled across the grass a light went on in the downstairs office. Flynn rushed to the window just in time to see them disappear into the trees. There was a commotion of shouting from inside the house but the girls didn't hang around. There was no plan, they just ran. Sophie's heart was in her mouth as they tore through the trees, stumbling occasionally when their feet got caught up in the undergrowth.

'Stick to the overgrown areas,' Sienna said, as they climbed up a steep incline. 'It'll make it harder for them to follow us.'

They paused at the top to catch their breath, listening to the silence and scanning the foliage below them.

'There's no sign of them at the moment,' Sophie whispered.

'They're bound to follow us,' Sienna answered.

They listened a while longer.

'I can't hear any barking,' said Sophie, 'so at least they don't seem to have any dogs.'

'We should do a ninety degree turn,' said Sienna. 'They'll probably expect us to keep going straight, so if we change direction we may be able to shake them off. This island's big enough for us to stay hidden for quite a while.'

Sophie looked up at the stars and calculated how to steer north. Fifteen minutes later they were almost at the coast. They found a dense area of shrubbery and crawled inside to rest.

'We should be alright here for a while,' said Sienna.

They sat without saying much for a short time, enjoying the stillness of the night after their frantic escape from the house. The waves crashed against the beach a short distance away but nothing else stirred.

'I'd love to have a look at the papers in this briefcase,' said Sophie after a while, 'but I daren't use the torch on my phone. What do you think those two are up to?'

'Well, if they're trying to develop mind control drugs that would explain why Julius Merrick is here. But why would he want to get involved with people like Flynn and Osorio?'

'And what was that list of names all about?' said Sophie. 'You don't think they're trying to influence The British Government do you?'

'It wouldn't surprise me,' said Sienna. 'Osorio would stop at nothing in his lust for power. Those files we saw could be a list of their intended targets. And if they managed to take over one government how long do you think it would be before they took over another, and another?'

They heard a speedboat patrolling out on the water. Sophie assumed it was Flynn's security guards watching for signs of them trying to make an escape.

'What do you think we should do?' Sophie asked. 'Uncle John's little boat isn't very fast. We could never outrun a decent speedboat. But if we're going to get this stuff back to the mainland we'd better do it before the sun comes up. At least at night we'd be harder to spot.'

'I'm not leaving without The Orb,' said Sienna.

'But they know we're here now,' said Sophie. 'They'll be watching for us.'

'I'm sorry Sophie, I'm not leaving. I came to your world to find The Orb and return it to its rightful place. Now it's within reach I can't back away.'

They sat in silence for a while. Sienna crawled out of

the bushes and lay on her back staring up at the stars. She was deep in thought. After a while, she suddenly sat up.

'I think our best bet is to split up,' she said, rejoining Sophie inside the bushes.

Sophie froze with terror at the thought of being left on her own.

'What?' she said. 'I'm sorry Sienna, I'm not sure I can do this by myself.'

'Of course you can. Look, if we stick together and we walk into a trap they've got both of us. But if they only manage to catch one of us there's still a chance they can be defeated.'

Sophie bit her lip and looked at the sand.

'So what are you suggesting?' she said, trying to be a bit more upbeat.

'I'll start working my way back towards the house. It'll be the last thing they'd expect. If I can catch Osorio unawares I might be able to grab The Orb and make my escape. In the meantime, you can start making your way back to where we've hidden the boat.'

'And then what? If I'm spotted by the speedboat I'll have no chance.'

'True,' said Sienna. 'But I'll bet they only have one

speedboat. And it must take them at least fifteen minutes to go right around the island. So if you set off a few minutes after they pass you, it should give you the chance to get to the mainland without being seen.'

Sophie thought about it for a few seconds, then she turned to face Sienna.

'You know what? That might work,' she said.

'Well, it's certainly worth a try,' Sienna answered. 'If you can get the briefcase back to the mainland it will be all over for Flynn and Osorio. Do you think you can drag Betsy back into the sea by yourself?'

'Looks like I'm going to have to?'

'Right, I'm going to get started,' said Sienna. 'See you in a while Little Sister.'

Sophie leaned forward and gave Sienna a hug.

'Take care Warrior Queen,' she said.

Sienna moved off quietly through the bushes and headed back towards the house. Once Sophie was alone she became aware of the silence again. A solitary cloud obscured the moon momentarily and the island was bathed in darkness. She felt isolated and vulnerable and wondered whether she could actually pull this off.

How had she become involved in something so dangerous? There could be armed guards hunting for her right now and last night someone took a shot at her. These are not nice people. And what will become of the country if she doesn't manage to get the briefcase back to the mainland? She felt a rush of fear but quickly tried to stifle it. It was no good staying here. Something had to be done. There was no alternative but to go back to the boat and try to make it to the mainland.

Checking her watch, she calculated it would take another ten minutes for Sienna to reach the house. She crawled out into the open and headed off around the coastline to where they'd hidden Betsy earlier. There were plenty of bushes and shrubs to give her cover so it was fairly easy to stay hidden and still stay close to the shore.

A sudden thought flashed into her mind. Sienna had stored some small bottles of water on the boat before they hid it in the bushes. This really lifted her spirits. After her earlier exertions a cool drink would be very welcome right now. She could almost taste it.

But as she approached the spot where they'd hidden the boat she stopped dead in her tracks. She heard the sound of voices, followed by a loud banging noise. Peering out from behind a large bush she saw two of Flynn's security guards. One of them had a small axe and he was hacking a hole in Betsy's hull.

Sophie's heart sank. This was a crushing blow.

The other guard spotted the bottles of water. Sophie looked on in horror as he opened them up and tipped the contents out onto the sand. Then he took out a two way radio and spoke into it, laughing from time to time. He seemed triumphant that he had disabled the girls' escape route.

What was she to do now? She felt totally devastated. Sienna was at the other side of the island and there were security guards searching for both of them.

The speedboat powered away from the beach, bouncing up and down on the waves. Once it was a fair distance from the shore, Sophie emerged from behind the bush and crossed over to where Betsy had been vandalised. There was a large hole in the hull, it would sink within seconds. Slumping down beside the boat, she put her head in her hands and tried not to cry. She was tired, thirsty and feeling rather dejected. She sat there for some time just staring at the sand. It all seemed so hopeless. She wanted to crawl under a bush and hide there until morning. But she knew in her heart there was no alternative but to follow Sienna to the house.

Even though it was still dark, the dawn chorus started to filter through to Sophie's ears. The birds of the island were the first to rise and their song welcomed the start of another day. Their voices were filled with such optimism it raised Sophie's spirits a little, enough for her to realise she'd already done more than she ever thought was possible. She had been through a lot and yet still survived.

Gathering herself, she thought about her options going forward. It was time to put a more positive spin on things. The girls were up against several armed guards and two power crazed maniacs, but so far they'd managed to outwit them all. And by cutting off any chance they had of retreating, the guards had unwittingly empowered the girls even further. Sophie now realised they would either have to win or perish.

The first thing she decided to do was to try to send a telepathic message to Sienna. There was no way of knowing whether it would get through to her but it was worth a try. She sat for a few minutes and focussed her mind. She had to let Sienna know about Betsy.

The next thing to do was find some sort of weapon. Sophie had never been in a fight in her life so she had no idea whether she could actually hit someone. She thought about what it might be like and whether she could actually go through with it. What if she was faced with her own possible death? Could she do something then? And could she do something violent to save Sienna?

There were some large rocks scattered around which looked like they could inflict a nasty wound, but that would entail getting close enough to someone to be able to use them. So they were discarded. Next she found a stout branch that must have been dislodged from a tree in the wind. It was about four feet long and the thickness of her wrist. This was perfect.

The only other thing that needed to be done was to hide the briefcase. It had to be somewhere recognisable so she could easily find it again. She scanned the landscape for the highest point around and headed towards it keeping a watchful eye out for security guards. About thirty metres from where Betsy lay was a large Hawthorne bush. This was the perfect landmark. Finding a spot underneath the Hawthorne, she put the briefcase on the ground and covered it with bits of broken bark and leaves. Now, at last, she was ready for what lay ahead.

CHAPTER 18

As Sophie crossed the island for the second time the sun was creeping slowly above the horizon. It was a new day with new possibilities. Heading east, it felt as if she was walking out of darkness into the light.

The sky had softened to blue and it was good to feel the warmth of the sun on her skin again. She'd survived two dangerous nights already. Someone must be watching over her.

It had been some time since she'd eaten or slept, and having lost the bottles of water that were stashed on the boat, her mouth and lips felt parched and dry. Stopping to rest at regular intervals she tried to conserve as much energy as possible. If a sudden emergency occurred it would be important to still have a little strength left.

In the massive expanse of woodland that covered the island, she was aware that she was a stranger. This was not the domain of people. The whole area was teeming with life but in the stillness of the morning, very little of it was visible. She felt so isolated and out of place. Every step she took seemed unnaturally loud.

But her thoughts were suddenly interrupted when she sensed some movement up ahead to her right. She stopped dead and silently waited. In a clearing about thirty metres away she saw it again. A large bush rustled as if someone had barged against it. What were the guards doing in the heart of the island? How could they possibly have found her? She was a needle in a very big haystack. She moved off to her left where there was another large clump of bushes. The guards may not have noticed her yet. If she could find somewhere to hide they might just pass her by.

The next few seconds were utterly chaotic. Just as she reached the bushes a figure burst from behind them, knocking her forcefully to the ground. She let out a cry, shocked by the suddenness of it and landed face down in the coarse woody debris of the woodland floor. Winded by the attack and terrified of what was to come she turned to face her attacker again, but all she saw was the hind quarters of a large deer disappearing into the trees. The startled animal didn't look back. It sprinted across to the clearing to join the other deer who were feeding on the lush foliage of the woodland. Sophie rolled over onto her back and exhaled loudly in relief. Another lucky let off. She was starting to feel quite blessed.

About a hundred metres from the house she sat down and leaned back against a large tree, taking in a deep breath of the damp morning air. She looked at the heavy branch she was carrying. Could she really smash this into someone's head? A host of other thoughts raced through her mind. Where was Sienna? Had she managed to find The Orb? Was she OK?

The security guards knew the girls were still on the island because they'd found the little boat. But hopefully, they wouldn't be expecting them to return to the house. It was even possible that most of the guards were out looking for them right now.

She sat for a moment and tried to send a telepathic message to Sienna. She had to let her know she was here. Then she focussed her mind again in case it was possible to pick up any response Sienna might send back to her. It was a long shot. But maybe she could be subtly influenced without actually knowing it. What to do next? Perhaps she should move a little closer to the house. It would be easier to decide on her next move once she knew whether anyone was up yet.

In daylight, the buildings looked completely different. The old house was still intact, even though it was a little dilapidated in parts, but a large outbuilding had been built alongside it and now occupied the bigger part of the plot. It looked more like a factory than part of a house and the silver grey material it had been made out of looked quite out of place in this picturesque setting. It could easily have been a giant space station built to accommodate an alien invasion. A helicopter was parked some way away from the outbuilding on an area of land that had been cleared of vegetation.

There was no sign of Sienna. A lone security guard was sitting on a chair in front of the outbuilding reading a newspaper. It was all very quiet.

A man appeared at the door of the house and walked across the grass towards the trees. Sophie recognised him immediately. It was Julius Merrick. He stopped about twenty feet away from where she was hidden and stared at the ground intently. Something was troubling him. A few moments later, Flynn came out of the house and joined him on the grass. Merrick looked at him and shook his head in disgust.

'Do you have to follow me out here as well!' he shouted.

'Look Merrick,' said Flynn. 'It's a fairly simple choice. You can either work with us on perfecting this drug, or a member of your lovely family might end up having a serious accident.'

'You need psychiatric help,' said Merrick. 'You know that, don't you?'

'No, I need your help,' said Flynn, 'so get on with it. Either make your choice or I'll make it for you. And that won't be good news for your family.'

Merrick lunged at Flynn and tried to grab him around the throat but he wasn't quite quick enough. By the time he'd steadied himself for another go, the security guard was on the scene and Merrick's arm had been twisted up behind his back.

'You've got until nine o'clock,' said Flynn, pushing his face up close to Merrick. 'If you haven't started work by then, my friends on the mainland might be paying your family a visit.'

As Flynn stormed off the security guard pushed Merrick to the ground. He sat there for a few minutes rubbing his shoulder and staring at the grass. He looked as if he was about to cry.

Sophie wondered whether she should reach out to him but she wasn't sure how this could help. The most important thing to do was to find Sienna, then get the briefcase safely back to the mainland.

She decided to circle around to the other side of the outbuilding to see if there was any sign of Sienna. But then something made her backtrack to the rear of the house. She didn't know why, it just felt like the right thing to do.

She saw Osorio first. He was holding a gun and he was pointing it at Sienna. On seeing them Sophie realised why she'd felt compelled to go to the back of the house. She must have picked up a telepathic message, a cry for help. She needed to act fast and make a difference. There was no time to sit and think about it.

They were too far away for Sophie to launch an attack. She had to think of a way to get Osorio closer to her. Instinctively, Sienna made a move towards the bushes where Sophie was hiding. Osorio followed, pointing the gun at her and smiling malevolently.

'Oh yes, please run and give me a reason to kill you,' he said. 'Then I can send your body back to your weak and feeble father as a present from me.'

He was now about six feet away from a tall holly bush facing towards the house. Sienna knew that his mind was powerful enough to pick up Sophie's thoughts. She needed to keep him fully occupied while Sophie tried to edge within striking distance.

'You think my father is weak?' she shouted. 'You're the one who needs a gun to protect you from a girl. Perhaps that's why my father was able to defeat your pathetic plan to take over?'

'Silly child, the war isn't over yet,' he answered. 'Once Mr Flynn and I have finished our work here everyone will do exactly as we tell them, you included.'

Sophie was edging closer to Osorio's back. She could feel the tension building inside her. Her mouth was dry and her hands were starting to shake. She knew she would have to attack him. It was the only option.

'I'll never do anything you tell me to do you filthy vermin!' screamed Sienna. She was desperately trying to hold Osorio's attention as Sophie positioned herself behind the holly bush.

Osorio smiled and shook his head, unaware that Sophie was now within striking distance.

'Oh yes you will,' he said. 'Once the drug is inside your veins you will do exactly as I bid. And you're the one person who can get close enough to your father to kill him. You see my dear child, by coming to this world you have handed me victory after all.'

Sophie closed her eyes and put every ounce of strength she had into swinging the large branch at Osorio's head. The loud thud it made as it thwacked against its target sent a shudder through every part of her body. It was a sickening sound and she needed a moment to steady herself. Then she remembered that her life was in danger and they needed to get out of there. When she looked up Osorio was lying face down on the ground. Sienna was kneeling beside him rifling through his pockets. She found The Orb, kissed it, and put it in her pocket. Then she took Osorio's gun and rushed over to join Sophie in the bushes.

CHAPTER 19

Osorio stirred, rolled over onto his back and rubbed his head. Pulling himself up onto his knees, he scanned the surrounding bushes. The girls didn't hang around. They ran back through the trees never looking over their shoulders. As they tore through the vegetation that surrounded the house, they could hear a commotion of noise coming from behind them. This time they knew they would be followed. It was a good five minutes before they paused to catch their breath.

'So they've sabotaged our boat, have they?' Sienna asked, as they crouched low behind some bushes.

It was a while before Sophie could answer.

'Yes,' she said, still trying to catch her breath. 'So how do we get back to the mainland now?'

They saw some movement through the trees about fifty metres away. Osorio, Flynn and two security guards were giving chase.

'We'd better get out of here,' said Sienna.

They headed towards the southern coast where the ground was higher and would give them a view across the island. If they could find a high point it might be easier to defend. At the very least they'd be able to see whoever was approaching. The sun was now blazing in the sky and it was hot and heavy going. Just as they thought they had shaken off their pursuers, a bullet hit the rock above their heads and shook them into a new sense of urgency.

Sienna pulled out the handgun she had taken from Osorio. She held it at arm's length and took aim for several seconds. Then she slowly squeezed off a shot. It hit a tree just to the side of Flynn and all their pursuers threw themselves to the ground.

'We should split up again,' said Sienna.

Sophie's eyes widened in alarm.

'You must be joking,' she answered. 'What's the point in that?'

'Look, I've got a gun so at least I can defend this position. If I can draw their fire and take them with me, there's still a chance you can get those papers back to the mainland. But if they corner both of us, it's all over.

Then there'll be nobody to stop them carrying out their plan.'

A series of shots were aimed in their direction. Crouching down behind some rocks, Sienna noticed that a security guard was rapidly advancing towards them using the bushes to provide cover. She steadied her arm and fired another shot. This time it hit the man directly in the chest and he fell to the ground. Sophie gasped at the brutality of it. The reality of what was happening finally started to sink in. Either the girls would have to kill all of their attackers or they would be killed themselves. She started to shake.

Another shot rang out and this time it hit Sophie on the arm. She cried out in pain. It had come from behind a large rock over to their right. Sienna took careful aim, steadying her hands and waiting. In the split second the guard emerged again from behind the rock she let off another shot. It tore through his throat and sent his body tumbling down the rocky incline.

When she saw the second man die so brutally, Sophie thought she was going to throw up. She stared at her bleeding arm in shock, unable to take in what was happening. Sienna leaned over to examine the wound. She took off her bandana and handed it to Sophie.

'Hold this up against the cut,' she said. 'It'll help to stem the bleeding.'

Sophie just stared at her blankly. Sienna shook her other shoulder.

'Sophie, you've got to do something about the bleeding. Come on,' she pleaded, shaking her again.

Another shot hit the rock just above their heads. This seemed to bring Sophie to her senses. She took the folded bandana off Sienna and held it against her arm. Her clothes were splattered with blood. She was feeling weak and in pain.

'There's a path over there that looks like it could take you down to that clump of trees,' said Sienna. 'If you can make it down to there, you could circle around the island and find somewhere to hide while I hold this lot off.'

'I can't leave you here,' said Sophie.

'You have to. Please Sophie, you have to go.'

They had been reunited for such a short time the last thing Sophie wanted was to be on her own again. But she realised Sienna was probably right. Somehow they had to get those papers back to the mainland.

She reached out and touched Sienna's hand. They exchanged a brief smile then Sophie left. As she picked her way down the makeshift path, she could hear more shots being exchanged and Flynn's creepy voice shouting out to the girls. Sienna was right. One of them had to make it back to the mainland to make sure these two maniacs didn't get away with whatever evil plan they had in mind.

By the time she was halfway down the path, she heard another barrage of gunshots. She wondered how many bullets Sienna had left. Then she gasped in horror when she realised Flynn was circling around behind Sienna. A few more steps and he'd have a clear shot at her back. She had to do something to help. Putting her fingers between her lips and using all the strength she could muster, she sent out a shrill and high pitched whistle. Sienna spun around and sent a shot at Flynn. It caught him on the top of the leg and he fell to the ground.

As Flynn lay on his back he looked across to where the whistle had come from. When he saw a figure standing there, he fired off a shot. It hit the tree next to Sophie and ripped a lump out of the bark. She didn't wait around for him to get a better aim but set off through the trees, desperate to find a hiding place. Despite the wound to his leg Flynn struggled to his feet and trailed after her, almost oblivious to the blood that was seeping down his trouser leg into his shoe. He was fuming with anger that two girls had been able to cause such disruption to his plans and he intended to make them pay.

Exhausted, frightened, and needing to find somewhere to rest, Sophie moved as quickly as she could. Fortunately, Flynn's leg injury had slowed him down considerably so she was able to put some distance between the two of them quite quickly. She found a dense collection of shrubs and large bushes packed closely together and crawled into the middle of them trying not to leave a trail.

A few minutes later Flynn limped into the clearing just in front of where she had concealed herself. His face consumed with anger, he was holding the gun and scanning the area frantically. Sophie held her breath, praying he would pass right by. He came within a few feet of her then he paused. The silence was terrifying. Nothing was moving. Even the wind had momentarily stopped. She fought to remain calm and keep herself from panicking, even though her heart was beating intensely against her chest and her hands were starting to shake. He stayed in one spot for what seemed like an eternity, breathing erratically and muttering to himself inanely. Then finally he turned and limped away, staring at a spot further down the path.

Her relief was so overwhelming Sophie thought she was going to cry. She bit her lip and tried to focus on staying calm. Every step Flynn took as he slowly shuffled away released more tension from her body. It was a miracle she hadn't been discovered. But then Flynn paused for a moment. He stayed completely still swaying on the spot, then to Sophie's horror he turned and started walking slowly back towards the spot where she was hidden.

He stopped by the bushes, still muttering to himself. Sophie held her breath hoping her stillness could somehow make her invisible. Flynn poked the barrel of the gun through a gap in the foliage, then moved it to one side so he could get a better look inside. She could see his eyes. They were jerking around like crazy, unable to focus on any image for very long. For a second they seemed to settle on her face. A faint hint of recognition flickered through him. Then inexplicably he turned and started limping slowly away again, scanning the undergrowth on either side for a clue to her whereabouts.

CHAPTER 20

For a few moments, Sophie just sat and stared into nothing. How could he have missed her? He was looking straight at her. She took a deep breath and watched Flynn as he shuffled further and further away. Her arm was aching and the sleeve of her jacket was heavily blood stained. She peeled back the fabric where the bullet had ripped through her sleeve and looked at the wound. She had been lucky. It had only caught the side of her arm and the bleeding now seemed to have stopped. But at the sight of all the dried blood she had to inhale sharply to stop herself from passing out.

Once Flynn was out of earshot she took out her phone and tried to call John, but she couldn't get a signal. She crawled out of the bushes. It was now vital to get right away from here. Find somewhere to hide until she could work out how to get back to the mainland. It was important to move quickly. It was the one advantage she had over him. And the island was so densely populated with trees and bushes, if she could get a long way away from Flynn she could make herself almost impossible to find.

But her heart stopped when she looked into the distance. At the top of the cliffs, about a hundred metres ahead, she could see the figures of Sienna and Osorio. They were squaring up to one another and they both looked poised to attack. Sienna had her knife drawn. Osorio was brandishing a length of wood. They were circling one another cagily, very close to the edge of the cliff. Sophie knew she was too far away to be able to help. All she could do was watch and pray that Sienna's warrior skills were enough.

Osorio attacked. Sienna countered with her knife and slashed him to the side of the neck. Osorio landed a blow on Sienna's shin. She leapt backwards, clearly in pain. Suddenly they were at close quarters, wrestling and trying to land blows. Osorio's elbow clattered against Sienna's jaw, causing her to stagger for a moment. Sophie watched in horror as Sienna's knife slipped from her grip, bounced on the grass and plunged over the cliff. Now it was down to pure strength. The wrestling continued. Osorio had one hand around Sienna's throat and she looked to be struggling for breath.

The next few seconds seemed to happen in slow motion. In an effort to get both hands around Sienna's throat Osorio shifted his position, but in doing so he lost his footing. Both of them were so intent on winning the struggle they were unaware how close to the edge of the cliff they were, and as Osorio stumbled slightly, he slipped and fell over the cliff dragging Sienna over with him.

Sophie watched helplessly as their bodies cartwheeled through the air for an eternity, floating down the side of the cliff as if they were made of paper. She wanted to rush to the spot and catch Sienna before she hit the ground. Gather her up and whisk her away to somewhere safe. But it was too late. Their bodies crashed to the ground at the base of the cliff with a thud, then lay there motionless. Sophie felt as if her heart had been ripped out. For a few moments, she stood there in shock, unable to believe what she had just witnessed.

'Sienna!' she cried out. But she knew there was nothing she could do to help her friend now. Sienna couldn't hear her anymore.

But one person could. Flynn heard Sophie's shrill cry

of pain. He spun around on his good leg and looked back to where it had come from. The sound of Sophie's voice lifted him again and gave him a new sense of purpose. A demented smile flickered across his face. He limped back the way he came, closing in on his prey once more.

It took a moment for Sophie to gather herself, then she realised that Flynn could have heard her cry out and was probably on her trail again. Tears were streaming down her face as she rushed back inland, trying to get as far away from her deranged pursuer as possible.

She couldn't believe Sienna was gone. This had all seemed like a glorious adventure when they first set off in Betsy last night. Nothing terrible could happen because she was with Sienna. But now the reality of what they were doing wasn't exciting or romantic anymore. It was brutal and harsh. People were dead. Sienna was dead. It didn't seem possible. And Sophie knew that unless she was able to get away from Flynn and find a way back to the mainland, she could soon be dead as well.

Once she was well inside the cover of the trees she changed direction again, hoping to throw Flynn off her trail. If she could find somewhere a bit higher up, with plenty of lush vegetation, she would get a chance to rest and think about what to do next. Eventually, after about half an hour, she found a low hill with a cluster of thick bushes halfway up. She crawled inside and lay down to rest.

The sun was now full in the sky. It had been over twelve hours since she'd taken a drink or eaten anything, and she hadn't slept for twenty four hours. She lay under the bushes for a considerable time frightened and tired, trying to deal with her loss. Her Warrior Queen was gone. Now she was alone. How was she ever going to get off the island without Sienna?

Every now and again she dozed off for a couple of minutes but something always jolted her awake again. She wasn't thinking straight. Her mind was full of doubts. For the first time since she'd arrived on the island she was beginning to think she might never make it back to the mainland.

Finally, after a few hours had passed, she realised this wasn't a helpful way of thinking. How would Sienna have dealt with this? What would her next move have been? She decided she would have to take a risk. Her only chance of getting clean water to drink was back at the house. And the only way to get back to the mainland would seem to be on the speedboat, which was probably moored near the house. She would have to go there and take her chances. If she was going to die on the island it was better to do it whilst fighting to survive, than to waste away hiding under a bush.

Checking the wound on her arm didn't raise her spirits much. It looked horrible, but at least it hadn't started bleeding again. She tried to use her phone but still couldn't get a signal. Finally, after struggling out from under the bush, she made her way slowly down the small hill.

To raise her spirits she thought about what Sienna had said about being frightened. Sometimes you have to do the thing that scares you because it's the right thing to do. Sophie knew that if she could just get back to the mainland and lead John to where the briefcase was hidden, then maybe Sienna wouldn't have died in vain.

Making her way through the undergrowth she began to feel a little more optimistic. The rest had done her a lot of good. She felt energised and ready for the challenge that lay before her. But she had only been walking for a few minutes when she heard the sound of someone laughing. She stopped dead. About twenty feet to her right, with his back against a tree, Flynn was sitting on the floor smiling like a madman. He was still holding onto his gun and he was pointing it at Sophie.

'Well, well, well,' he said. 'Look what the Gods have brought me now.'

Her eyes flitted about looking for a quick escape route but there was no obvious cover nearby. Her heart sank.

'Looks like it's just you and me now sweetheart,' said Flynn, smiling insanely. 'Oh yes, I saw your little friend lying at the bottom of the cliff, and I knew that if I was patient eventually I'd track you down as well.'

Sophie realised she was now staring death in the face. She felt an impulse to cry and plead with Flynn, tell him she had no idea what she was getting into. But she quashed that feeling as soon as it surfaced. She was determined to stand tall and face this moment with dignity. Meeting Sienna had taught her there was another way to live, a better way, a more courageous and fulfilling way. She stared back at Flynn as he struggled to his feet and shuffled across to where she stood. He had clearly lost a lot of blood and was having great difficulty walking, but he looked triumphant.

'Don't think this is the last of it, Flynn,' said Sophie defiantly. 'Our friends and family know where we are and they'll be coming after us.'

Flynn laughed hysterically.

'Well, this is the last of it for you sweethe

'If your friends are coming to the rescue th

hurry up.'

'You think you're going to take over don't you?' she said. 'We saw that list of politicians you drew up and your plans to develop mind control drugs.'

'Yes, but your little secret is going to die with you, isn't it?' he said.

'Maybe,' said Sophie, 'but we took the briefcase with all your papers in it. It's hidden somewhere on the island. When our friends search the island and find that briefcase you're finished.'

Flynn's mouth started to twitch. He glared at Sophie and pointed the gun directly at her head.

'Tell me where that briefcase is,' he shouted. 'Tell me now.'

'Or what?' said Sophie defiantly. 'Or you'll shoot me? You've already told me you're going to kill me, so why would I give up the one thing I know could still bring you down?'

Flynn's eyes flitted around distractedly. A crazy smile broke out on his face.

'Look,' he said. 'I'm sure we can come to some agreement here.'

'OK,' said Sophie, 'maybe we can.'

'Yes, of course we can,' said Flynn, trying to sound reasonable.

'Alright,' she said.' You take me back to the mainland and once I'm safely back inside the hotel I'll tell you where I've buried the briefcase.'

She stared at his face defiantly. It took a moment for Flynn to realise what Sophie had said then he began to laugh in fits and starts.

'Oh very funny,' he shouted. 'You think you're very clever don't you little girl? Well let me tell you, there's nothing clever about dying for something that's none of your business.'

He lifted the gun again and trained it on Sophie's head.

'Last chance,' he shouted. 'Tell me where that briefcase is.'

There was a crazed look in his eyes. He was close enough for Sophie to be able to look down the barrel of the gun. She could see his finger on the trigger. He started to gently squeeze. Despite her earlier bravado, Sophie knew she was now about to die. She was barely breathing and her whole body had started to shake. Flynn's finger curled a little more tightly to apply greater tension to the trigger, and then suddenly Sophie heard a loud *thunk*. It wasn't a sound she associated with a gunshot but then she'd never had to die before. It felt like she was in a dream.

She looked across at Flynn. His eyes had rolled back into his head and were now just showing the whites. He swayed on his feet momentarily, the arm holding the gun now hanging limply by his side. Then he fell forward like a plank of wood and crashed to the floor face down. Sophie looked with astonishment at his prone figure spread-eagled on the floor and gasped at what she saw. A knife with a carved handle was sticking out of his back just below his shoulder blade.

CHAPTER 21

For the next few seconds, Sophie was in total confusion. A host of thoughts stampeded through her mind. She wondered whether this was what the moment of death was like. The most pressing problem you're faced with suddenly disappears and you're free again, free to dream. Your imagination runs wild. In the split second that you pass from this world perhaps everything you want is suddenly bestowed upon you in one final moment of true happiness.

She stood for what seemed like an eternity staring at the lifeless figure on the ground, trying to take it all in. Flynn hadn't fired the gun. She was still alive. Somehow she had managed to survive. Then she started to become more aware of her surroundings.

Some movement in the bushes rustled the leaves a little and was followed by the sound of someone coughing. Approaching the bushes cautiously, Sophie peered around behind them and the sight she was greeted with threw her emotions into total confusion once more. Sienna was lying on the ground clearly very badly injured. On seeing her battered body, Sophie felt the tears well up in her eyes. She knelt down next to her unable to believe what was happening. When Sienna didn't stir, she touched her face and Sienna opened her eyes and smiled.

'Is he dead?' she said.

Sophie looked back towards the lifeless figure of Flynn.

'Yes, I think so,' she answered. 'Did you throw the knife?'

Sienna nodded and smiled, then exhaled and closed her eyes again.

Sophie was struggling to find the right words to say.

'I saw you go over the cliff. I thought you were dead.'

'So did I,' said Sienna, opening her eyes again. 'But it obviously wasn't meant to be.'

'I'm so sorry,' said Sophie, wiping tears away from her eyes. 'I just left you there. I should have gone to help you.'

'No, you did the right thing,' said Sienna.

'No, I didn't,' said Sophie, slumping to the ground next to her. 'I should have at least checked to see if there was something I could do. I'm so sorry Sienna. I'll never be able to forgive myself.'

The tears were streaming down Sophie's face. Sienna reached across and took her hand.

'Look, we knew that one of us had to get back to the mainland,' she said 'so it was best that you went inland and tried to hide. And you don't need to apologise to me. You're a good friend and I'm very glad that you're here.'

Sophie smiled through the tears and squeezed Sienna's hand. She dried her eyes on the sleeve of her jacket and tried to compose herself.

'What about Osorio?' she said. 'What happened to him?'

'When I woke up he was gone,' said Sienna. 'And so was The Orb. He's probably gone back to the house to get the rest of the guards so we'd better get away from here.'

She tried to sit up. The effort made her wince with pain. Sophie inhaled sharply when she saw Sienna's left arm. It was hanging at a strange angle. It had obviously been broken in the fall. Sienna noticed the anguished look on Sophie's face.

'I think my arm took the brunt of the impact,' she said. 'In fact, the whole of my left side feels quite battered. I'm just glad I fell onto the sand or it could have been a whole lot worse.'

Sophie helped her to her feet. Then she put her arm around Sienna's waist and the two friends started walking very slowly away from the area.

'Wait,' said Sienna, stopping suddenly. 'I want my knife. And we'd better get Flynn's gun as well. We'll probably need it if we encounter Osorio.'

'I'll get them,' said Sophie.

She searched around for a spot where Sienna could rest.

'Why don't you wait over there, under that oak tree,' she said.

Whilst Sienna sat with her back against the tree, Sophie moved quickly back to the spot where Flynn lay. She knew that she would have to take the lead from now on. Sienna was relying on her, and this time she wasn't going to let her down. How could she have left Sienna at the bottom of the cliff? The thought of it still gnawed away at her. If only she could go back in time and change the past, but she knew that wasn't possible.

She scanned the surrounding vegetation for any sign

of Osorio and the guards but saw nothing. The important thing now was to make sure they both got back to the mainland. By some miracle, Sienna was still alive, and Sophie was determined that no matter what happened she was going to lead them both to safety.

When she reached Flynn's body he was exactly as they had left him. This was the first time Sophie had ever seen a dead body close up and at first she was frozen with fear. It was definitely Flynn's body but some of the vitality seemed to have gone from it. It looked like an empty shell. She bent down and pulled the knife out of his back. It took quite an effort. The sight of all the blood and the eeriness of the scene were making her feel faint. She thought she was going to throw up. Quickly wrenching the gun from Flynn's clammy fingers she ran back to where Sienna sat and dropped the knife and gun on the ground. Then she rushed into the bushes and threw up what little food was still inside her.

When she crawled back to where Sienna was sitting, the knife was clean again and Sienna was examining the gun.

'It's empty,' Sienna said, as Sophie sat down beside her.

'Empty?' Sophie answered. 'You're joking.'

The memory of staring down the barrel of the gun was still so clear in her mind. She'd really believed she was facing the moment of her death.

'So he couldn't have shot me anyway.'

'He couldn't have shot you and, judging by the state of his leg, he couldn't have caught you if you'd run away either.'

'Do you think he knew it was empty?'

'Probably not,' said Sienna. 'He looked a bit demented when he was pointing that gun at you. The loss of blood and the heat must have really got to him.'

'That might explain why he didn't see me in the bushes,' said Sophie. 'He was looking straight at me, and then for some reason he just turned and walked away.'

Sienna tossed the gun aside.

'We should go,' said Sophie. 'Do you think you can walk?'

'I'll give it a go. Let's try to work our way back towards the house. They'll have water there, and it might be the one place they wouldn't think of looking for us.'

The sun was now high in the sky and despite trying to keep to the shaded areas the girls found it tough going. They were both dehydrated and desperately in need of a rest. They also hadn't eaten since the previous evening. It didn't take much effort for their energy levels to slump. Every step was a massive effort.

They had to stop at regular intervals to rest and gather themselves again, and by mid afternoon Sienna was finding it harder and harder to get back up. Finally, as they rested under a large beech tree, Sophie realised that Sienna was totally exhausted.

'I can't go on Little Sister,' she said. 'I've got nothing left.'

'But we can't wait here,' said Sophie

'I know we can't. But I can't go on either.'

Sophie sat and stared at Sienna. Her Warrior Queen looked completely drained. All the fight seemed to have gone from her. She reached out her hand and gently touched Sienna's right shoulder. Sienna closed her eyes and surrendered to sleep.

It was late afternoon by the time Sienna stirred again. As she became aware of her surroundings, she tried to sit up but then gasped and grabbed at her left arm.

'Have I been asleep?' she muttered, wincing through the pain.

'Yes,' said Sophie. 'I'm sorry I didn't wake you, but I thought you'd need your strength back if we're going to have a chance to get home again.'

'But you must be exhausted as well,' said Sienna.

'Yes,' said Sophie. 'But I didn't fall off a cliff.'

'Oh yes, I forgot about that,' said Sienna, smiling.

'Wow, that was almost a joke,' said Sophie, smiling back at her.

After the terrifying events of the last twenty four hours, it was comforting to have a bit of light relief. Things still looked fairly bleak, but being back in Sienna's company had definitely lifted Sophie's spirits, even though it was upsetting to see her so badly injured.

They weren't smiling for long though.

'What was that?' said Sienna suddenly.

They heard the sound of voices, men's voices, and it sounded as if they were approaching the spot where the girls were hiding.

'Oh no,' said Sophie. 'How did they manage to find us so quickly?'

Struggling to their feet, they dodged sideways into a thick clump of bushes hoping desperately they hadn't already been seen. They looked at one another for a moment, both aware of how limited their options were. Sienna was badly injured and would never be able to outrun the guards. If Osorio managed to catch her alive her father's life would be in terrible danger. Their only hope was to keep perfectly still and pray that the guards passed them by.

'Give me your knife,' Sophie whispered.

'I can't,' Sienna answered. 'If they see that you're armed they might shoot you on sight. It's me they're after, you should make a run for it.'

The voices were getting a lot closer.

'I'm not leaving you again,' said Sophie. 'We're going to see this thing through together.'

She picked up a rock. It wouldn't be much use against a gun, but it was all she could find and she had to do something.

Suddenly someone was standing by the bushes they were hiding behind. They could see his boots through the gap at the bottom. A hand pushed through the leaves, parting them, and then a face appeared. When he saw the girls he called out to the others.

'I've found them, they're over here,' he shouted.

They heard the sound of feet rushing through the undergrowth towards them. Perhaps it would have been easier not to resist, but Sophie was determined to stand and fight even though she knew it might be futile. She'd been through so much in the last two days that she was beginning to find an inner strength. The odds were massively stacked against them. But they'd survived their death once already that day and Sophie was intent on doing it once again.

When the man suddenly appeared at the side of the bush Sophie gasped in shock. Standing next to him was the mysterious stranger from the hotel and he was carrying a gun. She jumped in front of Sienna to shield her. They weren't going down without a fight.

'Who are you?' she shouted, brandishing the rock. 'Why have you been following us?'

'Don't worry,' said the mystery stranger. 'We're here to help.'

The girls looked at him in confusion.

'Oh, thank heavens you're alright,' said a voice to Sophie's left. It was a voice she knew, a voice that made all the fear drain out of her.

'Uncle John,' Sophie shouted, running over to him and hugging him in relief.

'It's alright Sophie,' he said. 'You're going to be OK now. These men are on our side.'

The mystery stranger knelt down next to Sienna and examined her arm.

'That looks like a bad break,' he said. 'How did you do it?'

'I fell off a cliff,' she answered.

He raised his eyebrows and whistled.

'Wow!' he said. 'You got away lightly then.'

He took off his shirt and made a few rips in the fabric, then tied it around her neck to fashion a makeshift sling. She winced and grimaced as he moved her arm to get the sling into position.

'I think this should keep your arm in a more comfortable position until we can get you to the hospital,' he said.

'Thanks,' said Sienna. 'Next time I fall off a cliff I'll give you a call.'

Sophie looked at Sienna and smiled.

'That's two jokes in one day,' she said. 'At this rate, you'll be working at a comedy club by the end of the week.'

'And it will be all your fault,' said Sienna, smiling back at her.

John opened his backpack and handed the girls a small bottle of water each.

'Sip it slowly,' he said 'It'll be too much of a shock for your body if you gulp it down in one.'

Never had water tasted so good. Even though it had been warmed by the afternoon sun, it still tasted like a cool mountain stream.

'Wow, that's good,' said Sophie, sitting down next to Sienna and clinking bottles with her.

'Girls, this is David Harrison,' said John, pointing at the mystery stranger. 'He works for the government. He and his men have been monitoring what's happening on the island for the last few months.'

'Is that why you were spying on the protesters?' Sophie asked.

'Yes,' said Harrison. 'We've had several agents working in the town for a while. James here is one of them.'

The other man nodded at the girls.

'We knew at some point Flynn would send some thugs in to disrupt the protests,' Harrison continued 'so we've been photographing them so we know just who we're dealing with. We've also had an agent working undercover as one of Flynn's security guards. He let us know that two girls were being hunted on the island, so we knew we had to move in and get you two out.'

'How did he manage to get through to you,' said Sophie? 'I've been trying to contact Uncle John since yesterday.'

'Yes, Flynn had a jamming device in operation as a security measure. But our man was left to guard Julius

Merrick when the rest of them went out hunting for you and he managed to turn it off long enough to phone me.'

'Flynn's dead,' said Sophie.

'Yes, we know,' said Harrison. 'We found his body as we fanned across the island. What about Osorio?'

'We don't know where he is,' said Sienna. 'When we heard your voices just now we thought it might be Osorio and the guards.'

Harrison took out his two way radio.

'I'll contact Control and let them know we've located you.'

But before he could make the call the man called James stepped forward and pushed a gun into Harrison's face.

'I don't think so David,' he said, leaning across to take the radio.

'What the hell…' said Harrison.

'We're all taking a trip to the house,' said James. 'Mr Osorio has plans for you lot.'

CHAPTER 22

They all sat for a few seconds and stared at James in shock.

'What's happening?' said Sophie, looking across at John.

'Well, it seems our friend James has been working for Flynn and Osorio all along,' he answered.

'Shut up old man,' said James. 'You might think you're great just because you were in the service a long time ago, but now you're just a flabby hotel owner.'

John visibly bristled, but there was a gun pointing at his chest so he had to just sit there and take it.

'You're a fool James,' said Harrison. 'You know how the department deals with people who turn against us.'

'When Mr Osorio is in charge there won't be a department,' said James, leaning forward and taking

Harrison's gun. 'Now shut up and get over there with the rest of them.'

He took another two way radio out of his pocket, still pointing the gun at Harrison.

'Hello base, this is Tango 2, over,' he said.

The crackly reply was audible to everyone.

'Tango 2, this is base. Go ahead.'

'Base, I've found the girls. I have two other guests as well. I'm taking them to the beach at Heron Point. Over.'

'Roger, Tango 2. We'll send the boat to Heron Point. Over and out.'

He slipped the radio into his shirt pocket and took a step back.

'OK everyone, on your feet. We're going for a little walk. And remember, if either of you guys is tempted to be a hero, one of the girls takes a bullet.'

As they trooped off towards the beach Sophie felt totally dejected. For a brief moment she'd thought the nightmare of the last twenty four hours was over, but now they were right back in trouble.

Harrison and John led the way, then Sienna and lastly Sophie. Her feet were aching from the amount of ground she'd covered over the last two days and the heel of her right foot had become badly inflamed.

'You two girls had no business getting involved in this,' James shouted as they marched towards the beach. 'You should have stuck to your pop music and make up.'

When they reached the beach there was still no sign of the boat, so James marched them over to some large rocks and told them to sit down and wait. Sienna was still having difficulty moving and Harrison had to help her to the ground.

Sophie took off her boot. When she slid down her sock to examine her foot she found the heel was red and swollen and a large blister was starting to form. She looked inside her boot. There was plenty of sand in there. Those small grains rubbing against her heel must have caused the damage.

After a few minutes, they could hear the boat in the distance but it hadn't yet come into view.

'Right, on your feet,' said James, pointing the gun at John and Harrison.

Sophie knew she had to do something. The boat would be here any minute and she couldn't allow Sienna to be taken back to Osorio. Before putting her boot back on she tipped the dry sand out into her hand. Then as she got to her feet she brought her hand up in a fluent motion and flung the sand into James's face.

He stumbled backwards, temporarily blinded. That was all the time that John needed. He covered the six feet between himself and James in a split second and battered him with a series of savage blows. The attack was brutal. Within seconds James was lying unconscious on the sand.

Harrison grabbed the guns and gave one to John.

'Nice work old man,' he said, smiling. 'You haven't forgotten much since you left the service.'

'Some things you never forget,' said John. 'Great work with the sand Sophie, I never saw that coming.'

'Neither did I until I was standing up,' she answered.

'The best ideas often come at the last minute,' said Sienna. 'Great move, Little Sister!'

The sound of the boat was getting nearer. Harrison grabbed James's body by the shoulders and dragged him back over to the rocks.

'We'll sit him up against this rock with his back to the sea,' he said. 'Make it look as if he's still in charge. Anyone approaching from the sea won't be able to tell that he's out cold. Then once they're within striking distance we can make our move.'

They all sat down again as if nothing had happened.

Seconds later the boat rounded Heron Point. When it was close enough for them to see who was on board, they couldn't believe their luck. There was only one guard on the boat.

'Right,' said Harrison. 'Everybody stay calm. Let's just see what he does next.'

Nobody moved. They knew they had to get him onto the beach before they could do anything. They sat there and waited. Finally, the guard climbed off the boat and waded through the shallow water towards the shore. Sophie noticed he was carrying his gun in a holster. Clearly, he wasn't expecting any trouble. He reached the beach and started walking towards them. She was surprised at how close they were letting him get. Soon he was only about thirty feet away. She knew she had to stay calm and act natural. Finally, when he was only about ten feet away, he stopped and scratched his head.

'OK, let's get this lot onto the boat,' he said, lazily.

She couldn't believe the plan had worked so well. It hadn't even occurred to the guard that this might be a trap. But then, quite unexpectedly, James' body slumped to one side and collapsed onto the ground in a heap.

When the guard realised what was happening he tried

to draw his gun, but before he could reach it John charged into him and knocked him to the ground with a grunt. Sophie looked on in horror as they rolled on the sand in a wrestling fury, each trying to get a hand on the gun. A few terrifying seconds passed. John hadn't lost any of his combat skills. He landed a couple of heavy blows with his free hand and the guard seemed to realise it was hopeless. This wasn't worth dying for. He'd had enough.

'OK, OK,' he shouted, giving up the fight.

Harrison immediately contacted the mainland and ordered his agents to move in on the island. It was a massive relief to know that help was finally on the way.

As they waited to leave the island, Sophie took John to the spot where she'd hidden the briefcase earlier in the day. It was only a short distance away and they found the Hawthorne bush quite easily. Then they walked a little further and found the vandalised wreckage of Betsy.

'I'm so sorry Uncle John,' said Sophie, looking at the massive hole in the hull.

'Don't worry about Betsy,' he said, smiling at her. 'I'm just glad that you're OK. There are plenty more boats in the world, but there's only one Sophie Watson.'

Sophie smiled and gave him a hug. Then they walked back to the beach to meet up with the others.

Before long they heard the choppy sound of a helicopter approaching in the distance. It landed on the wet sand further down the beach, blasting the vegetation close to the shore with a sandstorm.

Once they were cleared to take off again Sophie, Sienna and John were lifted into the air and the helicopter headed north, on course for a military base on the outskirts of Dorchester.

Gazing down at the island Sophie felt totally numb. The girl who had arrived in Bramlington Bay just a few days ago was not the same girl who was now high above the trees. The old Sophie, the cautious and hesitant girl from Hampton Spa, had been left behind on the island.

Two days ago, on the rain soaked country roads of Dorset, the warrior inside her had been awakened. Though her first tentative steps may have been hesitant and unsure, the last twenty four hours had shown Sophie just how powerful she really was. She felt as if she had shed a skin. And through her friendship with Sienna, she'd learned that there was a better way to live, a more courageous way. No longer would she allow her fears to hold her back.

As they flew low over the tops of the trees, Sienna glanced out the window and for a few seconds, she thought she caught sight of Osorio. He was standing in a clearing holding The Orb in the palm of his hand and smiling up at the helicopter. She knew it was his way of saying 'I am still in control. I will be victorious.' It was a bitter pill to swallow. But she also knew that she was lucky to be alive and she was glad of the chance to fight another day.

It was only when the helicopter had touched down at the military base that Sophie would allow herself to believe the battle was finally over. It was such a massive relief she could feel the emotion welling up inside her. It was hard to talk. She felt elated but totally drained.

A team of medics started treating the girls as soon as they arrived, dressing their wounds and fixing a support splint around Sienna's broken arm. The nurses seemed to be aware of everything the girls had been through and were full of admiration for what they'd achieved.

When John came to see them a short while later, they had already settled into a double room in the hospital wing and were enjoying something warm and comforting from the canteen.

'I suppose I should be angry with you for going to the

island in the first place,' he said. 'But what you two pulled off last night took incredible courage. If those two maniacs had been able to perfect their mind control drugs it would have been very serious indeed. They could have taken control of the British military and our security services, which would have affected the safety of the entire world.'

'Have David and his men found Osorio?' Sophie asked.

'I'm afraid not,' said John. 'He seems to have completely disappeared.'

Sienna exhaled loudly and shook her head in frustration.

'He could be anywhere by now,' she said. 'With The Orb he can travel between worlds. But he'll surface eventually and I'll be there waiting for him.'

'They've rounded up all the security guards though,' said John. 'And Julius Merrick is now safely back on the mainland.'

'He wasn't on their side,' said Sophie. 'They were blackmailing him. Flynn threatened to hurt his family if he didn't cooperate with them.'

'Yes, he told the agents that when he was rescued. And apparently Flynn and Osorio were very close to being able to use those mind control drugs, so you got there just in time.'

The nurse arrived and tried to usher John out.

'The girls need some rest,' she said. 'You can come back to see them later.'

He stood up to leave, then turned back towards the girls and smiled.

'And there's one other good thing to have come out of this,' he said. 'With Flynn no longer around to threaten the council members, it's now very unlikely there'll be any more development on Kestrel Island. So, thanks to you two, the protest movement has been a huge success.'

A big smile spread across Sophie's face. She couldn't wait to tell her mum that the island was now safe. But whether she'd be happy to tell her the whole story she still hadn't decided.

The nurse appeared at the door again and looked disapprovingly at John. He flashed a smile at her, but she responded by holding the door open a little wider. He got the message.

'OK girls,' he said. 'I'm going to leave you to rest. I'll come back to see you later if there's any more news.'

Once John had left they lay there in silence for a few

minutes. It wasn't necessary to say anything. They were just enjoying being in each others' company.

After a while, Sophie looked across at Sienna and chuckled to herself.

'I suppose this is what it's like when you have to share a bedroom with your big sister,' she said.

'Yes,' said Sienna. 'You both end up needing hospital treatment.'

Sophie burst out laughing.

'Good one,' she said. 'I wish I'd thought of that.'

Sienna smiled back at her, happy to be able to make her friend laugh.

'Do you think we'd have fought if we'd been sisters?' She asked.

'Well, it looks like we'll be here for a few days,' Sophie answered, 'so we'll soon find out.'

Also by A.B. Martin

Under Crook's Wood

A strange creature has been spotted in Crook's Wood on the outskirts of Hampton Spa. Was it just a trick of the light or is there something more sinister and dangerous going on? There's certainly something odd about Heath Grange, the mysterious ramshackle house on the edge of the wood.

When Sophie and Sienna decide to investigate, they may have bitten off more than they can chew. There are dark forces watching their every move and the girls might be walking into a trap.

Who is eccentric Professor Felso and what is his underground secret?

Can the girls keep their heads above water and make it back to town before disaster strikes?

Or will power-crazed Osorio plunge the country into chaos?

Sophie and Sienna are back in another action-packed adventure that moves at a breathtaking pace and keeps you turning the pages.

Available now at your favourite online bookstore.

If you enjoyed this book…

Thank you so much for checking out Sophie's adventure on Kestrel Island.

If you enjoyed reading the book, I'd be very grateful if you could spend a minute leaving an honest review on your favourite online bookstore. Even one short sentence would be very much appreciated.

Reviews make a real difference to authors. They help other readers get a feel for the book, and I'd also be very interested to hear your thoughts on the story.

Thank you for your help,

A.B. Martin

Acknowledgements

Many thanks to Roisin Heycock for her insightful edit that helped me shape my manuscript and get the best out of the story. Also to Dane at ebooklaunch.com for the wonderful cover design.

And a special thank you to my wife, Annie Burchell, for all the support she has given me while I've worked to get this book published. Without her ideas, thoughtful and detailed advice and constant striving for excellence this story may never have been told.

About the author

A.B. Martin is an English author who writes thrilling middle-grade adventure stories and intriguing mysteries.

Before becoming an author, he wrote extensively for television and radio and performed comedy in a vast array of venues, including the world famous London Palladium.

Kestrel Island is the first book in the Sophie Watson Adventure Mystery series. It was published in 2017.

Under Crook's Wood, the second in the series, was published in October 2018.

He lives in London, England, with his wife and daughter.

Printed in Great Britain
by Amazon